The Curse of the Hanging Tree

TULSA

ISBN: 978-1-957262-35-2 (Paperback)
The Curse of the Hanging Tree

Copyright © 2022 by Alan E. Losure
All rights reserved.

No part of this publication may be reproduced, distributed, or transmitted in any form or by any means, including photocopying, recording, or other electronic or mechanical methods, without the prior written permission of the publisher, except in the case of brief quotations embodied in critical reviews and certain other noncommercial uses permitted by copyright law.

For permission requests, write to the publisher at the address below.

Yorkshire Publishing
1425 E 41st Pl
Tulsa, OK 74105
www.YorkshirePublishing.com
918.394.2665

Published in the USA

The Curse of the Hanging Tree

Alan E. Losure

Other Books by Alan E. Losure
Available at Amazon.com

Quest for the Truth
My Desperate Journey
Murder… in a small town
Murder Returns… to a small town
Death Comes Calling… in a small town
Terror Strikes… in a small town
Where Angels Fear to Go
Death Is No Stranger
Death Walks Among Us
The Mystery of the Tolling Bell
Death Takes No Holiday
The Copycat Killer
The Adventures of Tommy the Drummer
Boy (children's book)

I wish to dedicate this book to the memory of my friend and number-one supporter, ex-mayor of Gas City, Larry Leach. Larry stood by me during my early years of writing historical fiction stories and encouraged me to continue with his many suggestions, encouragements, wisdom, and love for the history of our town.

Gas City is now a much better place to live thanks to Larry Leach.

"I find television very educating. Every time somebody turns on the set, I go into the other room and read a book."
Groucho Marx

Note to my readers: If you are a fan of my other stories, you will notice that this first story takes place a few years earlier than during the time frame of my last few books. I just hated to give up on the exciting time of the 1890s, when people owned horses and not Honda's. The short second and third stories are a sneak peek of the new characters I've developed. I hope you will enjoy them as well.

Alan E. Losure

The Curse of the Hanging Tree

Main Cast of Characters:

Roscoe Sawyer	Grandfather
Vivian Sawyer	Grandmother
Wilma Sawyer	Older Spinster Daughter
Anita & Frank Collins	Parents of Stanley & Julie
Stanley Collins	Mentally Challenged Son
Julie Collins	Daughter
Daniel Slagle	Neighbor Farmer
Thaddeus Rains	Grocer
Cynthia Rains	His Daughter
Matthew Rains	Brother of Grocer
Felix Abbott	Neighbor
The Young Stranger	The Stranger
Hershel Bancroft	Businessman
Charlie the Rag Picker	Hermit
Roland Edwards Sr.	Businessman
Olive (Mother) Edwards	Wife of Roland
Roland Edwards Jr.	Son/Businessman
Violet Edwards	Wife of Roland

Alan E. Losure

Sandra Lawrence	Edward's Family Cook
Floyd Talbott	Businessman
Justin Blake	Marshal of Gas City
Virginia Blake	Wife of Justin
Wilbert Vance	Deputy Marshal
Rachael Vance	Wife of Wilbert/Mother
Mary Louise Vance	Young Daughter
Michael Davidson	Deputy Marshal
Doris Davidson	Wife of Michael
Tracy Stevenson	Friend and Mother
Brother Jacobs	Member of the Shakers

Modern Day Characters:

Paul Middleton	Owner of the Ledger
Tonia Middleton	Wife of Paul
Wanda Westland	Gas City Historical Society Volunteer
Cecil Beck	Gas City Historical Society Volunteer

Early Main Street view of Gas City, Indiana

CHAPTER 1

Present Day Springtime

What would YOU do if you were in possession of a terrible old secret? A secret passed down from generation to generation that, so far, had remained unknown except for a selected few. That was a question Paul Middleton had begun to ask himself throughout the years after receiving the old ledger book from his elderly mother. She had stressed the need to remain faithful as its new keeper. "Be very selective as to whom you show it to," she had urged. "As my mother explained, its disclosure would bring great shame to others." That weekend, he began to read, and after doing so, he set it aside on his top closet shelf. *Quite interesting, but I don't see how it can hurt anyone today. All those people are dead,* he told himself. The old ledger remained in place and was soon forgotten.

Paul Middleton was a retiree from the General Motors plant in Marion, Indiana. He and his wife Tonia lived in the small town of Van Buren and were the parents of three adult children and four active grandsons. Then last fall, Paul decided to repaint the interior of their bedroom closets before the cold weather set in. Tonia hated the smell of paint, so nice weather was needed for a cross breeze from their open windows. After removing everything from his closet, Paul noticed the old ledger. *I think when we have the family here for Christmas, and everyone is settled comfortably in the living room, I'll send the grandkids off to the bedroom to play with their new toys, and then share the contents of the old ledger and get their reactions.*

The months passed by and finally, on a snowless Saturday, December evening, the family gathered together for their traditional Christmas dinner. Tonia had spent many hours preparing the large meal but it was quickly consumed. The ladies worked in unison and soon had the remaining food packed up in the refrigerator and the dirty dishes placed inside the dishwasher. Their grandsons were quite anxious for presents to be opened that were packed tightly under the illuminated Christmas tree. All too soon it was over as the adults admired their new gifts while the children played with their new noisy toys.

Paul instructed the grandkids to go off to play on the other side of the house. "I have something I wish to read to all of you adults if you don't mind," he said. "It's an old ledger that's been passed down within my family, its historical contents kept a closely guarded secret. I would like to take some time and read it all to you. So, get comfortable and give me your full attention. Afterward, I want your opinion as to whether it should remain hidden away or publicly shared." He then began to read aloud.

Forty-five minutes later he was finished. A general discussion resulted from each member as the ledger was passed around. All the men agreed there was no need for it to remain secret any longer, while two of the daughters expressed some general concerns. One of the sons-in-law turned to his wife and joked, "Now that explains a few things I've wondered about you!" There was no laughter from anyone in the room, and the look he received back from his wife told him his joke wasn't appreciated. Not by a long shot, and he knew he'd hear about it after the couple left for home.

To break the remaining chill in the air, the youngest daughter expressed a more thorough opinion. "It's not like anyone today will be hurt by it." She went on to say that the faded hand-written text was hard to read. "You gotta admit, they sure had eloquent penmanship back then," she said. "But Dad, if you decide to go public, why not let me take it home and start typing it in Word on our computer? I could use a good weekend project this winter anyway. I'll make several copies for you as well. Then if you choose not to show it to anyone, easier to read copies will at least exist for the future." That seemed like a good idea and the old ledger was sent home with her. Several months passed before she returned to visit from her home in Ohio, and brought the ledger and a stack of copies. "The words were a great deal harder to make out than I expected them to be, but I got it all typed out just as it was written. Have you decided on going public yet, Dad?"

"Yes. Your mother and I have discussed it. We don't want the newspapers to get hold of the story, nor have it discussed on the internet. But there's one solution; over in Gas City is a historical museum that might be interested in having the ledger, since it does involve their history. What do you think?" Their daughter said it was worth a try. Paul took the ledger and one of the copies and placed it on his dresser. "Grab your purses, ladies. I'm taking you out for lunch in Marion at Applebee's." Nothing further was mentioned as they enjoyed their daughter's rare company until later that evening.

CHAPTER 2

A Decision is Made

The following Saturday afternoon, Paul found the Gas City Museum's telephone number on their website and placed a call to ensure they were open. They were, a man had said. Paul then collected the materials to take with him. "Are you sure you don't want to come along? You could walk through their museum while I speak with the volunteers," Paul said to his wife. Truth be told, he was both a bit nervous and excited at the same time, hoping he was making the right decision.

Tonia shook her head. "No, I want to start cleaning those dirty windows out in the sunroom. You go ahead. I'm sure I'll visit the place one day."

Paul tossed the old ledger and papers into the front seat of his car and backed out of their garage. He enjoyed the short drive over to Gas City. The weather was pleasant and sunny, slightly on the cool side, but a welcomed relief from last winter's heavy snows. He had a vague idea of the museum's location just a couple of blocks off the highway through town. Passing under the I-69 overpass, he couldn't help but notice all of the new businesses and restaurants that had opened over the last few years. *Someone thought ahead and made plans for this area's growth,* he thought. *Too bad Van Buren hadn't.* Once in town, Paul continued on Main Street until noticing a small sign indicating a right-hand turn to the museum. After parking on the street across from the museum, Paul was immediately reminded of the old Van Buren School he attended that had been demolished many years ago. The museum was located inside an old school building once called West Ward. It too had a familiar item on its east side; a large, round fire escape slide. During his youth, Paul and his friends often climbed and slid down the old high school's fire escape that connected to the upstairs study hall. Paul gathered up his materials and approached the front doors. Setting outside the entry stood a large antique wheeled fire extinguisher. *I wonder why they put that thing there?*

Entering, he came upon the building's wide stairs leading up to the top floor. The sound of "ding-dong" emitted from a floor-mounted security device indicating someone had entered. The image of small children climbing those stairs long ago flooded his mind. *If only this old building could talk.* At the top of the stairs, Paul could hear voices coming from the large room on his left. Outside its entrance sat a large display case. Entering the room, he was met by a polite hello from a man sitting at a long table. "If you wouldn't mind, we would appreciate you signing the guest register," the man said. Paul picked up the ink pin lying on the open page and provided his

The Curse of the Hanging Tree

name and address. He noticed that so far that day, he was their only recorded visitor. Across from the man sat a lady looking intently at a computer screen. Both were volunteers of the historical society. "Is this your first visit to our museum?" the man asked rising from his seat to greet the new visitor.

"Yes, it is," he replied as he looked about, quite impressed at all he saw. "I see that you have a wide variety of historical artifacts from your town's past, and that's why I'm here today. My name is Paul Middleton, and I live in Van Buren. My folks originally came from Gas City, and lived here in the late 19th and into the early 20th century."

The man seemed interested in helping. "Perhaps we might have a written record of their names in our records."

Paul smiled. "I'm betting you do. You see, my great-grandfather was your chief of police. His name was Wilbert Vance." Upon hearing this, the lady left her computer and approached.

"That's a name we certainly recognize," she offered. "My name is Wanda Westland and this old coot here is my friend Cecil Beck. We're volunteers of the Gas City Historical Society. We'd be happy to share anything we have in our files about your ancestor. As you may already know, he was a deputy marshal under Marshal Justin Blake. When Blake left office, your ancestor was chosen to fill his vacancy. Vance then changed the title for the office to the more modern term chief of police." From the look on their visitor's face, it was clear that this information was already known.

Paul was now ready to state his true business for being there. "What I have here is an old ledger compiled by him in 1931, just shortly before his death. In it, he tells of a terrible secret kept quiet all these years. We discussed it over Christmas, and I came to the realization I should speak with you folks. My daughter even typed the long story out for easier reading. If you are interested in hearing it and have the time, I'd like to read it to you." Paul paused to await their reaction.

"Yes, by all means. We'd love to hear it. Anything historical only adds to our town's wonderful history. Let's sit down at this table and make ourselves comfortable," Wanda said. "May I offer you something to drink? I have some coffee in my thermos."

Paul shook his head. "No, but thank you anyway." He could feel a breath of excitement in the air as he composed himself. Both of the volunteers sat patiently waiting for him to begin. Paul took hold of the thick stapled pages lying on the table before him. "It starts with a handwritten cover page that my daughter made a copy of," he said as he began to read out loud.

> June 11, 1931
> Gas City, Ind.
>
> Allow me to introduce myself. My name is Wilbert Vance and I am the past chief of police here in town. Something terrible occurred when I was working as a deputy marshal while serving under my best friend, Marshal Justin Blake.

I have kept the following facts a secret for all these years, something that I am not proud of and haunts me as I sleep. I fear now that if I don't put the truth to paper, it would be forever lost, as my health is not good. I hope that when I am gone, those who come after me will read this and come to understand the very difficult decision I had to make back then. I will leave it up to you to decide what you would have done if you had been in my place. As I understand it, the story began like this...

Wilbert Vance

CHAPTER 3

May 7, 1885

Farmer Roscoe Sawyer, wife Vivian,
Grandchildren Stanley and Julie

"So, I guess that completes everything," Wells County, Indiana, farmer Daniel Slagle said after completing the purchase of Roscoe Sawyer's neighboring farm. The sad old man only nodded as he recounted the stack of bills, and inserted the stack into his pocket. "Roscoe, my friend, I will hate to see you and Vivian move away, but I understand your family's situation." Roscoe looked upon his friend's face with visibly watering eyes.

"Dan, we hate to go," Roscoe said. "I've worked this land for many years and built a home for us. But yes...our situation has certainly changed. I can't think of anyone else I would rather hand my land over to, old friend."

The men offered their hands and each assumed they wouldn't see each other again; they were more than neighbors, having been good friends for many years. "Take your time in moving out. I'm sure it will be difficult for all of you to leave your home of many years," Dan suggested.

"You and Rebecca were wonderful people to know," Roscoe said without thinking. Slagle's wife Rebecca had died last year and Daniel had already started courting a local widow. Determined to change the subject, Roscoe said, "You know at my age, and with my bad back, it's getting more and more difficult for me to do farm work, and our daughter's offer to move to her boarding house in Alexandria is our only real option."

Daniel said he understood but he also realized there was far more to his friend's situation other than his age catching up to him. After saying a final goodbye, Roscoe mounted his horse and slowly made his way back toward their old farmhouse, as his mind drifted back to the dilemma that had changed their life.

During the last two years, Roscoe had felt like the weight of the world had been placed on his shoulders. But life hadn't always been this unhappy. Not by a long shot.

He and Vivian raised two wonderful daughters, Wilma being ten years older than Anita. Neither girl had shown any interest in living on a farm. When she came of age, Wilma moved to Alexandria, Indiana, where she answered an advertisement for a cleaning woman position at a local boarding house. Wilma eventually became good friends with the elderly owner, and when the old woman passed away, she was greatly surprised to discover she had been named the new owner of the boarding house, and along with it, a sizable savings account at the Alexandria bank. Wilma worked very hard to make her six-room boarding house profitable, clean, and a pleasant place for her tenants to live.

Anita, on the other hand, had married a boy named Frank Collins whom she went to school with, and the couple moved outside the small farming community of Warren. Her husband worked at all types of odd jobs as their family grew. A son, who was named Stanley, was the first to arrive, but the baby had been born with medical issues. The infant's umbilical cord had been twisted around the baby's neck, starving the brain of needed oxygen. As Stanley grew, it quickly became apparent that he would remain mentally a five-year-old child for the rest of his life.

On the other hand, daughter Julie had been a bright and outgoing child, two years younger than her brother. From an early age, Julie seemed to sense the special needs of Stanley and was quick to take his side with her parents and make excuses for his unfortunate shortcomings.

Life continued and remained challenging until two years ago when the unthinkable happened. The Collins's were living in a nice, two-story rental in Warren, when late one night, a fire broke out. Both children were sleeping downstairs and were able to escape before the place erupted into a blazing inferno. Many locals assumed that Stanley had been playing with matches and started the fire, but this was never proven. The children were now homeless and without parents; after the double funeral, they were brought to their grandparent's farm to live. Neither grandparent was prepared for the emotional challenges in dealing with Stanley.

The last two years had indeed been quite difficult. His grandfather hoped the boy might be able to help out with some of the chores, but this proved not to be the case, as the boy seemed to drift off into playtime. Sometimes he imagined himself to be an army soldier, other times, a cowboy or a wild Indian, with chicken feathers sticking in his hair. It was a sad situation that had to be endured, but both Roscoe and Vivian worried about who would take care of the boy when they were gone and hated the idea of saddling their spinster daughter Wilma with Stanley. Perhaps there was a place Stanley could one day be admitted. Some sort of hospital where they understood such things, Roscoe had heard tell of. Julie continued to be a great help to her grandmother and was wise beyond her young age.

As if all this wasn't enough, Vivian was beginning to act strangely, as her mother and grandmother had before her. Roscoe began to notice strange whispers emanating from his wife as if she was speaking to an unknown presence. This was the odd behavior he'd been told ran in the women's side of her family. Even Julie had noticed it and approached her grandfather one day out in the barn. Though she was only fifteen, Roscoe spoke with her about everything he was worried about. Julie became a full-grown adult woman in his eyes that day and each kept the other informed about her grandmother's strange behavior.

It all came to a head one March evening. Roscoe was sitting in his rocking chair while the women were washing and drying their evening dishes. After removing her wet hands from the dish pail, Vivian walked past him on her way toward the blazing fireplace, speaking in whispers and acting very strangely. At that point, she reached up and removed their family Bible that held a permanent place of honor on the mantle, and threw it into the flames. Roscoe leaped from his rocker and tried feverishly to fish it back out with the fireplace poker. He was successful in saving it from destruction.

"Why in the world did you do that?" he demanded to know. Vivian continued to whisper and giggle.

"They told me to do it," she replied.

"Who told you to do it?" he asked as he tried to wipe the soot off the Bible's cover with a wet washcloth.

"The spirits…are my friends, but they hate all of you!" She then walked back to the sink and began washing dishes as if nothing had happened. Both grandfather and granddaughter locked eyes, each now knew the truth without having to say it out loud. Something must be done about this, and soon.

* * * * * * * * *

Later the next day, Julie confided more of her fears to her grandfather. "I remember mother telling father she'd heard some form of madness ran on her side of our family. Will I end up like grandmother too?" She then began to cry.

"There, there, sweetheart, not if I can help it. Don't think those terrible thoughts. In my heart, I feel that won't happen to you. Last night's episode awakened me to the seriousness of your grandmother's condition, so I am going to write to your Aunt Wilma and explain what's going on. It's strange, your grandmother loves to read the Bible and it's not like her to do something like that. She needs to be seen by a doctor, someone who has a better understanding of these things. I'm hoping your aunt might suggest the proper answer." He then took pen and paper out into the barn and addressed all of his fears onto the pages. Roscoe then rode off into town to purchase a two-cent stamp and mailed the letter off to Alexandria. Now all they could do was wait, and hope for a reply. It came ten days later and read:

> Dear Father,
>
> Sell the farm and bring everyone here to live with me at my boarding house. Explain to mother that I need her and Rachel's help in exchange for free room and board. I will do all I can to help take some of the strain off of you.
>
> Love, Wilma

Though the thought of selling their home and farm was very painful to consider, Roscoe came to realize Wilma's suggestion was their only viable option. After speaking with his friend Daniel Slagle about putting his farm up for sale, he was immediately informed not to consider any offer until he had a chance to propose his own. That was exactly what Roscoe had hoped might occur. Convincing Vivian that Wilma desperately needed their assistance in operating her boarding house was difficult, but slowly the old woman came to terms with her husband's decision to sell out and move to Alexandria.

* * * * * * * * *

Several days later, the family was ready to begin their journey. Since Wilma's boarding house was fully furnished, there was no need to transport the family's furniture and most of their belongings, other than food supplies and cooking equipment. The family's freight wagon and pair of horses would be used, along with a tarp he'd fashioned overhead, as protection from the rain. This would allow the women to sleep in the wagon at night, while Roscoe and Stanley slept beneath it. He'd mapped out their way of travel and hoped to make five to seven miles per day. That should have the family arriving in Alexandria in around a week. With great sadness in his heart, but a determination to make this work, Roscoe Sawyer sped the team southward toward a new and hopeful beginning.

Spinster Daughter Wilma Sawyer
Aunt of Stanley and Julie

CHAPTER 4

Three Days Later

The weather had remained pleasant as the Sawyer family arrived days later just northeast of the outskirts of little Harrisburg. The Pennsylvania Railroad had lain tracks there back in '67 and there were hopeful signs that continued prosperity for the town would increase its size. "We're making good time," Roscoe said to his wife. "I think it wise to camp out here tonight. Harrisburg has a livery stable and I need to have that cracked spoke attended to before we go any further. Maybe a brief reprieve from the rigors of travel might be good for you and the grandchildren anyway."

Vivian nodded. "If you are going to be at the stable, the children and I will look the town over. We could use some more coffee beans anyway. Do you children want to go with Grandma or Grandpa?" In her eyes, her teenage grandchildren would forever be thought of as children.

Both exclaimed, "We want to go with you, Grandma!" Today Stanley was in his wild Indian mood once again, with chicken feathers stuck in his hair that he'd brought along inside his pocket. Though quite small compared to other towns, Harrisburg did have a mixture of stores and shops that Julie couldn't wait to enter. As for Stanley, this was as if a new, exciting world had materialized right before his eyes. He couldn't wait to see that big iron horse his grandpa told him about that makes its way through town, and perhaps, if he was lucky, to even touch it when it stops to rest.

After arriving outside the livery stables, Roscoe instructed that everyone was to meet back there, as fixing the spoke would take longer to accomplish than shopping. The blacksmith came outside just after the family had departed and approached the new arrival.

"Can I help ya?" the younger man asked.

"Yes, I sure hope so. Do you have time to look at my left rear spoke? I noticed it's cracked."

"Sure, bring your wagon inside, friend."

"I hope you'll be able to fix it rather than needing to replace the entire wheel. It only needs to hold together long enough for us to make it to Alexandria," Roscoe said. The liveryman was skilled in his trade and set to work replacing the cracked spoke while his family walked the town.

* * * * * * * * *

The excitement of being in a new wonderful location, full of stores and people overcame Stanley, as he became even more playful and loud than usual. Both women could see the concerned looks from storekeepers and fellow shoppers when Stanley started his Indian whooping and dancing. As a result, Julie was asked by her grandmother to stay outside and keep her brother entertained while she shopped. This disappointed the young girl immensely, and as hard as she tried, Stanley always seemed to break away from her and enter the shops anyway. Soon she gave up trying as the three of them continued to explore the offerings of the new town.

Vivian Sawyers' eyes soon located what she was looking for, a sign reading: **Hometown Grocery- Proprietor Thaddeus Rains**. His store was well known for displaying fresh fruits and vegetables while in season. Vivian motioned the way as the three entered the store. A woman with a small child was being helped at the counter by the grocer. The other person in the back of the store was a young man of about twenty who was looking over a pair of black leather boots. From the back room, a young girl of about sixteen years of age appeared carrying canned goods to restock the empty shelves.

All at once, every eye in the store focused upon the teenager with chicken feathers protruding from his hair, whooping it up, and hollering as if he was performing an Indian war dance. Vivian, who was quite used to people staring at her grandson's odd behavior, approached the counter. "May I help you?" the young girl asked as she glanced worriedly over at Stanley.

"Yes please, I'd like a half-pound of coffee beans," Vivian stated. To put everyone at ease, she then said, "Pay him no mind, dear. He can't help it." Everyone then realized the teenager's condition. The young girl moved toward the end of the counter to an open sack sitting on the floor, and using a metal scoop, filled it with coffee beans. She then began weighing them and added a bit more until the desired weight was achieved.

"For only a penny more I can grind them for you." Vivian had already noticed the large coffee grinder sitting on the counter, all ready for use. Realizing it would make her chore much easier than using the small hand-cranked grinder in their wagon, Vivian agreed. "I don't recall seeing you folks here before," the young girl casually mentioned.

Before Vivian could answer, her granddaughter replied. "We just arrived. We're from up near Warren and we are traveling to my aunt's boarding house down in Alexandria. My name is Julie Collins. This is my Grandmother Vivian Sawyer."

The young girl behind the counter smiled. "Hello, ladies. I'm Cynthia Rains. My parents own this store. Will you be staying in town very long?"

"No, I'm afraid not. Grandfather is having our wagon wheel repaired, and I guess we will camp out just northeast of town for tonight. We'll probably leave early in the morning. But maybe, if you like, I could come back after lunch so we can talk and get to know each other. I don't have much of an opportunity to speak with many girls my age."

"Yes, I'd like that very much," the salesgirl said. "I'll ask father for some time off. I was secretly hoping that you might stay around awhile, as I already know all the other girls in town." Vivian was pleased to hear that her granddaughter was making a new friend, even if only for a brief time.

During all of this, Stanley continued to whoop and holler until his eyes became fixed upon Cynthia. Stanley shouted, "Me big Indian chief. You my squaw!" He then made a grab over the counter toward the girl. Her father naturally became alarmed as Julie pulled her brother back.

"Hey, stop that! Leave my daughter alone!" he shouted.

"I'm sorry Cynthia, my brother can't help it," she whispered. Vivian hurried and paid for her purchase and motioned it was time to leave. She could almost feel the glaring eyes of the protective father, now happy they were leaving his store.

On his way out, Stanley turned and shouted, "You my squaw! I come back for you...you see...I come back!" The trio made their way toward the livery stable and waited until the wheel had been repaired, before venturing out of town to set up camp for the night. Vivian thought nothing more about it and didn't mention the incident to her husband.

* * * * * * * * *

After washing the lunch plates, forks, and skillet, Julie approached her grandmother. "Can you keep Stanley from tagging along behind me? I don't want him bothering us when I visit with Cynthia." Vivian agreed and instructed Stanley to stay behind and gather more firewood. Disappointment swept over the boy's face as his sister walked toward town and out of sight. The two girls met up and began enjoying their time together. "I can come back after supper if you want me to," Julie said to her new friend. It was agreed that the girls would meet out front after the store closed at six o'clock.

* * * * * * * * *

Right after supper, Julie made her way back into town, unaware that Stanley followed her in the distance. She arrived just as her new friend's parents were ready to lock up. Suddenly, Stanley appeared and began shouting, "Me big Indian chief. You my squaw!" Embarrassed that her friend's parents had heard him acting this way again, Julie forcefully ordered her brother to return to camp and to stop following her. He then appeared to do so.

"Let's walk and talk," Cynthia suggested, "I think I understand." All too soon it began getting dark and a full moon appeared overhead. With reluctance, Julie said her final goodbyes to her friend and made her way back to camp. Soon, the family was sound asleep as tomorrow promised to be another busy day of travel.

CHAPTER 5

The Late Arrival

It was nearly midnight when loud, angry shouting awakened the Sawyers to a group of men carrying a lighted torch approaching their camp. Roscoe crawled out from beneath the wagon and quickly got to his feet. "What's going on here?" he demanded.

"Shut up, old man! You know why we are here! Hand him over!" one of the men shouted.

"Where ya hidden' that dirty rotten scoundrel?" another yelled. "Ain't no good in tryin' ta hide, we'll find him!"

"There he is!" the younger man of the group shouted. "He's hiding under the wagon!" Three men then dragged Stanley out from under the wagon and onto his feet. The younger man stood holding a torch in one hand and a rope in the other, already fashioned into a hangman's noose. Each face reflected pure hatred and anger. By now both women had poked their heads out from the wagon's covering, as Vivian demanded to know what the fuss was all about. As soon as Roscoe saw the noose, he fought gallantly to protect his grandson but was outmatched by the other three men who beat him until he fell to the ground. Rising slowly, Roscoe felt intense pain emanating in his chest as he clutched his nightshirt in agony. The four men momentarily stopped and stared down at the old man who was no longer moving. Vivian leaped from the wagon and cradled her husband's head in her hands.

"You killed him!" she shouted. "Murderers'! Assassins!" Stanley momentarily broke away from their clutches and fell to his knees at his grandfather's side. They were joined by Julie as all three cried uncontrollably.

"It doesn't matter," the lynch mob's leader said. He was the grocer, Thaddeus Rains, joined by his brother Matthew, his next-door neighbor Felix Abbott, and the younger stranger holding the torch and rope. Thaddeus Rains nodded to the young man holding the noose. It was then draped around the head of Stanley. "Bring him!" Rains commanded as his eyes searched for the appropriate tree. "Over there. That one will do,"

Vivian Sawyer was now hysterical. "Why! Why are you doing this to us? We have done nothing to you people!"

After handing over the torch to another, the younger man threw the end of the rope over a solid, low-hanging tree branch. "That lunatic of yours strangled and raped my sweet daughter, Cynthia. The doctor doesn't know if she will live or not. We all heard him shouting that she was his squaw and that he'd come back for her. Well, he did and that young monster of yours has to pay for his terrible crime!"

Julie began pleading that her brother had the mentality of a small child and wasn't capable of such a hideous thing. Their pleading went unheeded as she huddled within the arms of her grandmother, each afraid to look any further. "Hand me that rope," Thaddeus Rains ordered as he pulled it tight and lifted Stanley off the ground. The helpless youth struggled briefly, but the terrible deed was soon over. Rains then released the rope's slack and the body fell beneath the branch of the tree. "It's done," he said with satisfaction in his voice. "Let's go home."

It was at that moment that the mind of Vivian Sawyer completely snapped. She began laughing in a strange, odious way and pointed her finger back and forth at each man. "All of you...all of you dirty butchers...I call upon the powers of darkness to curse every one of you! I curse not only you but those who will follow as well! I curse this hideous tree...I curse the very ground you stand upon! May it belch out black tears over its wicked soil! Go! Try to hide, but it shall do you no good! All shall perish for what you have done here tonight!" She then began shrieking; falling to her knees and scooping up dirt, in which she slowly poured back out to watch it fall.

"Let's get out of here. She's as crazy as that kid was." Thaddeus Rains said.

Julie Sawyer sat in shock the rest of the night after she encouraged her strangely quiet grandmother to return to the wagon. The young girl felt overwhelmed, unsure of what she should do next or how it was to be done. There was no way anyone in Harrisburg would help her now. Before her lie the bodies of her grandfather and brother. There was no shovel in their wagon and Julie knew she wouldn't be able to physically dig two deep graves anyway. By daylight, she'd made her decision. Using the tarp from the wagon, she covered the bodies of her family having pinned a note with each name to their clothing. Hopefully, they would be discovered and some caring party might perform a Christian burial. She then removed the money from the sale of the farm from her grandfather's pocket and placed it in her bag. It would be needed in the years to come. Though she had never hooked up a team of horses by herself before, she had watched it done many times before and successfully accomplished the task. With her now silent grandmother lying in the back of the wagon staring straight up into the air, Julie decided to head her team straight into Harrisburg. *I want them to see me and to know what an evil thing they've done to us.* She waited until another hour had passed so that more people would be out and about before entering the town. Slowly she rode through with fixed eyes staring straight ahead, wanting all to see her and to remember her final act of defiance. Afterward, Julie headed southward intending to ask along the way the directions to Alexandria. *Aunt Wilma will certainly have her hands full with us now,* she thought.

* * * * * * * * *

What was not known until later was that the unknown young man from the previous night's hanging party had left town sometime during the night.

Thaddeus Rains and his wife had sat by their daughter's bedside all that night praying for her recovery. Just before noon, Cynthia opened her eyes but seemed somewhat confused and her voice was very hoarse. Soon though she was alert and told her parents that a man had attacked her last night after she departed from her new friend, Julie Collins. "I don't know his name, Father, but he was in our shop yesterday looking at boots."

Greatly alarmed by this news, he told her she was confused. "It was that crazy kid acting like an Indian that attacked you."

"No, it was the young man from our store. You know the one who kept looking at me yesterday. Has he been caught yet? I remember he tried to kiss me and when I resisted, I felt his hands engulf my throat. I don't remember anything afterward." His daughter's statement floored Thaddeus Rains. *Oh my God... what have we done?* Motioning his wife to follow him out of the room, he told her he needed to go get his brother and neighbor and go search for the real guilty man. Nothing further was mentioned of the terrible crime that they committed the night before. Mrs. Rains strongly suggested that their daughter not be informed about the rape for now. The poor girl had been through enough already. Rains left to brief everyone on what he just learned. Matthew Rains and Felix Abbott were shocked to learn that acting out of haste had caused the death of an old man and the murder of an innocent youth, most likely incapable of such a hideous act. Knowing there to be no established law in town, the men split up and searched everywhere, learning from the stable boy that a young man fitting the description had departed during the night on horseback and disappeared into the darkness. Great anger swept through Thaddeus Rains that he hadn't asked the young man's name the night before and should have wondered why a stranger would willingly take part in a lynching. *He was most anxious that the kid was guilty and needed to be hanged,* he remembered.

That afternoon, Thaddeus Rains brought a freight wagon out to the scene of the hanging and discovered the identified bodies under the tarp. Retrieving the dead, he made arrangements for their burial in the pauper's section of the cemetery with simple gravestones. He heard later that a young girl driving a wagon was seen passing through town earlier that morning heading south. There was no point in trying to track the wagon down anyway. *The old woman was right. We are cursed and the memory of it will haunt me until the day I die.* One week later an exhausted but determined Julie Collins pulled up in front of her aunt's boarding house in Alexandria.

* * * * * * * * *

Cynthia Rains recovered physically from her terrible ordeal and learned of the rape. Unfortunately, loose talk around town was having a terrible effect on her mentally. She could see and sense people's eyes upon her. *They think I offered by body deliberately,* she worried. Word of the old man's death and the wrong youth lynched, as well as the old woman's curse, spread among the townspeople. This was due to the story being repeated by an intoxicated Felix Abbott inside a saloon. As a result, the Rainses saw a drastic drop off in business. Two weeks later, the hometown grocery store was put up for sale, and, once sold, the family moved to Kokomo to start their life over, away from local gossip. Shortly after arriving in Kokomo, Thaddeus Rains was instantly killed when he stepped into the pathway of a speeding streetcar. Matthew Rains was unable to attend his brother's funeral as he was confined to his bed, suffering from Pneumonia. He passed away a week later. Two months after, Felix Abbott's wife left him due to his excessive drinking and moved away. Abbott turned full-time to alcohol in attempting to quench his demons. It was not the solution to his problems, and he died soon after, a mere shell of his former self.

That fall, a violent storm erupted and a single bolt of lightning struck, splitting the infamous tree down its middle. The farmer who owned the land had a bad feeling about removing it and let the dead tree lay just where it had fallen. Townspeople later learned from a letter sent by the widow of Thaddeus Rains of his untimely death. That and the death of his brother, along with Abbott's situation, played into the story as people continued to refer to all that had happened as the curse of the hanging tree.

Chapter 6
The New Landowner

Hershel and Gloria Bancroft

The following year, the sixty-acre plot of farmland was sold to Marion businessman, and occasional oil speculator, Mr. Hershel Bancroft. He was unaware of the lynching that had taken place on his new property, and if he had, he would have used the terrible story to persuade the farmer to sell his property even cheaper, claiming it to be undesirable. But in truth, Bancroft didn't believe in the boogeyman anyway. His company, Bancroft Investments, planned to conduct expository oil drilling there; using men and equipment they had used before. A tall wooden derrick would be constructed, with the drilling accomplished by a small steam engine. With its expected success, their efforts should make him and his company's investors even richer. Hershel Bancroft had been married to his wife Gloria for twenty-three years. The couple had no children. Their home in Marion was quite nice by most people's estimates, but not nearly enough for him, as he was always seen contracting additional work to improve its outward appearance.

After inspecting his new property, Bancroft established the location where the new drilling rig was to be constructed, close to a fallen dead tree. "We are going to make out financially just fine," he told his wife. "Once we hit the gas belt, its pressure will force huge pockets of oil to rise to the surface where it will be collected in barrels, then taken to market. As for the natural gas, we'll just vent and burn it off. After the pocket is emptied, hopefully, many years from now, I will sell off individual tracks of the land for homeowners. Someday, I expect Harrisburg to extend their town's limits out that way. If we don't hit oil, then I'll just sit on the land and do nothing until it is profitable enough to sell as individual tracts."

The following week, work commenced on building the eighty-two-foot-tall wooden drilling rig, and within weeks, it was finished. The carpenters also constructed a modest size tool shed nearby to house their equipment and supplies. As for firewood for cooking meals, the men used the easy-to-access split dead tree lying close by. Once the drilling started, great care would be taken not to build their cook fires too near the rig, fearful of the possibility of escaping highly flammable natural gas seeping from the drill hole.

Hershel Bancroft, his wife Gloria, as well as his investment partners were on hand to witness the beginning of the drilling operation. The naming of drilling rigs was a common occurrence in the industry, so Bancroft, as the lead investor chose the name: *The Lucky Star*. "The Pennsylvania Railroad depot has a telegraph office within their terminal," he instructed the senior driller. "Contact us at once when you strike oil."

* * * * * * * * *

The following week, a team of familiar carpenters arrived at the Bancroft home to start the construction on an indoor bathroom addition. "We are too important now in our community to use an outside privy as common people do," he had said to her before scheduling the work. Mrs. Bancroft was delighted with the convenience an indoor bathroom would bring, especially during the winter. The workmen chosen were well known having worked on-site for the family's past exterior construction projects. Mrs. Bancroft insisted on baking cookies or having sweets on hand, along with coffee and tea to serve the men during a mid-afternoon break. The workmen greatly appreciated their employer's kindness and hospitality. And then, days later, it happened.

As the workmen arrived and were welcomed inside, they began to pick up where they left off the day before. Hershel Bancroft approached the men saying, "My wife noticed a small squeak in the new floor around where the bathtub will be installed. Here, let me show you." He then commenced standing on the area in question, rocking his body back and forth to produce the squeak. Without warning, one of the workmen took hold of a wooden mallet in one hand and then grabbed Mr. Bancroft tightly around the throat with the other. Before any of his co-workers could react, the attacker pushed the startled businessman down to the edge of their work area, and struck Bancroft's head repeatedly, causing it to burst open like a melon. The body was then released and dropped to the floor. Without displaying any emotion, the attacker dropped the blood-covered mallet and stepped back into the new addition, and began working as if nothing had happened. The other men rushed from the room, with one searching for a telephone to call the police, while the others made an effort to keep Mrs. Bancroft from seeing the scene of her husband's murder. After hearing the loud commotion; she tried to enter the room, only to catch a glimpse of the blood pooling on the floor. She screamed and fainted dead away.

The police soon arrived, as well as a doctor, but nothing could be done for the victim. After hearing what had happened from the startled workmen, the confused assailant was cuffed and taken into custody. He claimed to have absolutely no memory of attacking anyone. Despite the blood splattered on his white work coveralls, he continued to claim his innocence.

"I liked Mr. Bancroft!" he shouted. "You gotta believe me, I would never harm him or anyone else! I swear I know nothing about this! I am no murderer!"

* * * * * * * * *

Upon hearing the terrible news, Gloria's best friend Beth arrived to provide comfort as best she could under the circumstances. The ladies remained on the other side of the home and out of sight from the investigating police and the eventual removal of her husband's body. "I think I need someone to take me to the Western Union office. I must send a telegram to my sister, Sylvia Meadows in Indianapolis, and tell her what happened," she said. Beth telephoned her husband, and he immediately left to escort her stricken friend there and back. While Mrs. Bancroft was away, Beth attempted to mop up the blood, but was unsuccessful, as it had already begun to stain the new wooden flooring. After noticing a workman's drop cloth among the men's equipment, she used it to drape over the floor stain so as not to be seen.

Later that afternoon, a reply telegram arrived stating her sister and family would board the evening train to Marion and should arrive the following morning. Gloria Bancroft now knew that help was on the way. Beth had pleaded with her friend to spend the night in their home, rather than remain, but she had declined. She then offered to stay overnight with her, but again the offer was rejected. "I will be all right," she insisted. Beth stayed at her friend's side until the evening when Gloria said she now wanted to be alone. Reluctantly, her friend departed. The house now seemed strangely quiet as she made her way into the kitchen. She had not felt like eating all day and decided to consume an apple, rather than attempt a heavier meal. After finding herself wandering about aimlessly through her home, the widow climbed the stairs and prepared for bed. But sleep remained elusive as she lay trying to come to grips with everything that had happened. Though she had taken the doctor's prescribed medicine, she was unable to sleep and considered getting up to read. That had often worked for her in the past. Just as she crawled out of bed and inserted her feet into a pair of slippers, she thought she heard the sounds of strange, mournful chanting, far off in the distance. *It must be the wind,* she assured herself, returning an hour later and finally drifting off to sleep.

* * * * * * * * *

Her sister, brother-in-law, and teenage niece arrived the following morning. Beth's husband was on hand with his carriage to escort the family to the Bancroft home. The funeral for Hershel Bancroft was performed the next day and was heavily attended by businessmen and friends. Afterward, Gloria was encouraged to return to Indianapolis with her sister the following day. "You just need to get away for a few weeks, Gloria," her sister pleaded. "It will do you good and we would love to have you." Reluctantly, she agreed.

Gloria telephoned Beth and explained she had decided to accept her sister's offer to leave town for a needed rest. "Is there anything I can do for you while you are away?" Beth asked.

"Yes, I was getting to that," she replied. "I will leave a duplicate house key under the front floor mat. Would you mind asking your husband to hire a new crew of workmen to finish the bathroom project? The plans are still there in the empty addition. I don't want to have to deal with it when I return. I have already spoken with our banker to let you have whatever funds are needed to cover the cost from our...I mean my savings account."

Beth quickly agreed and said to have a safe trip. "I will see to everything, Gloria. I will miss you."

"I will miss you also. I will write you once I get situated, goodbye."

* * * * * * * * *

The next morning, the family boarded Bancroft's carriage and proceeded to the railroad depot to await the southbound train's arrival. Sylvia's husband then brought the carriage to the livery stable and explained that they belonged to Gloria Bancroft, who would be out of town for some time. "Please tell Mrs. Bancroft not to fret none about it. I will take good care of her horse and carriage while she's gone," the older man said.

Two days later a telegram arrived at the home of her sister addressed to Mrs. Gloria Bancroft, in care of the Meadows residence.
It read:
The Lucky Star struck oil.
Floyd Talbott

Chapter 7
Oil is Discovered

The Lucky Star Oil Well

Shortly after the funeral of Hershel Bancroft, the group of oil speculators met inside a local bar to decide who among them would replace him in representing their business interests. Floyd Talbott was soon chosen. Talbott was the natural choice as he was heavily invested in many properties, stocks, banks, and various railroads. Being a major stockholder in the Pennsylvania Railroad that serviced Harrisburg and Jonesboro, he had no difficulty arranging for the transportation of their new product to Indianapolis by rail. A team of workmen would fill fifty-five-gallon barrel drums full of oil, and then haul them to the loading dock to be placed into freight cars. The future appeared bright for the investors until it happened: the gas pressure dwindled to nearly nothing and the oil stopped flowing. *The Lucky Star* it seemed had become *The Fallen Star*. Apparently, the drilling had only reached a small pocket of subterranean oil. By the time Gloria Bancroft had returned home to Harrisburg, all of the drilling equipment had been removed from her property, and the rig site lay abandoned. No attempt had been made by the workmen to clean up the thick oil residue saturated under the abandoned derrick. Several townspeople remembered the old woman's curse, "May it belch out black tears over its wicked soil."

* * * * * * * * *

There is an old saying, "One person's loss is another's gain." That seemed to prove true for the man known locally as Charlie the Rag Picker. He had earned the nickname due to his occupation: going through people's discarded trash, looking for clothing, as well as any discarded items he might resell. Nothing was known about Charlie or his history, as he only appeared one day out of nowhere. He seemed a friendly, pleasant old fellow, and often people purchased his old rags and junk just to help him out. What few coins he managed to earn were quickly spent at one of the lower-class saloons down by the river. Fellow bar patrons gave him a wide berth due to his lack of personal hygiene. Charlie had discovered the abandoned derrick site and began to live in the small empty storage shed. On those days that he had acquired a few nickels in his dirty pocket, Charlie enjoyed being with other men at the saloon and started telling anyone who might listen, the strangest stories. Men would often buy Charlie a free beer just to keep him telling his tall tales of encountering the unexplained.

"I see strange lights and ghostly figure ah movin' about on moon-lit nights," he said. The men standing at the bar only smiled and occasionally chuckled. "Don't laugh!" he would say, "I also keep ah hearin' wild Indians chantin' and war whoopin' outside my shack!" Charlie's ghost stories were soon relayed to the men's wives and eventually spread around town.

Then one night in late fall, a large flame was noticed outside of town. The old wooden derrick was ablaze. Before it was finally extinguished, the flame had spread to the wooden shack. Later, the charred remains of Charlie the Rag Picker were removed and interned in a pauper's grave. It was assumed that a spark from his campfire or a carelessly discarded match had made contact with the accumulation of spilled oil known to lie beneath the derrick.

Soon, word of the tragedy reached the ears of landowner Mrs. Gloria Bancroft. She then offered the entire property for sale to businessman Floyd Talbot who had shown prior interest.

Taking advantage of the situation, Talbott was able to purchase the acreage at a great price. He made plans to have it surveyed in the spring and sectioned off into individual home lots. "I'm going to make a killing on this," he assured his fellow business friends. Then, the Panic of '93 struck the nation.

In February, the sudden and shocking news of the bankruptcy of the Philadelphia and Reading Railroad sent panic into the hearts of investors and the general public. Floyd Talbott had been a heavy stockholder in the company and overnight came close to complete ruin. He managed to stay afloat with a bank loan, listing all of his properties as collateral. That spring, the ground was sectioned off into housing plots and advertised for sale. Due to the economic situation, purchases were slow, with the choice locations nearest to town selling first. Greatly depressed with his financial situation, Floyd Talbott became somewhat of a recluse. Then, in May, his investments in the National Cordage Company, the largest rope maker in America, and a stock market favorite, disappeared as the company went into receivership. That day Floyd Talbott suffered a major stroke and lingered alone in his bed before passing away. The bank eventually assumed ownership over all his properties. Due to the economic slowdown, unemployment continued to rise, as citizens stormed local banks to withdraw their savings. Many banks, having loaned out more than they had on hand, closed their doors.

The late Floyd Talbott

That year, little Harrisburg officially changed its name to Gas City. A new uptown section of the town was built and plans were made to lay bricks on Main Street and extend the town's boundaries. A new, luxurious hotel was constructed called the Mississinewa Hotel. Also, a committee of businessmen calling themselves the Gas City Land Company was formed to offer free land and free natural gas to any factory willing to relocate there. Many soon did, providing much-needed employment to its citizens. Prosperity for the small Hoosier community soon followed. Though the location of the lynching of '85 and the lot next to it was as choice as any other, they remained unsold. Occasionally, teenagers would build a bonfire there at night with the hope of seeing and hearing something supernatural. Two more years soon passed by.

Then, in 1895, both lots were purchased by local businessman Roland Edwards Sr. to build a beautiful home for his wife, Olive, on one lot, while leaving the other undeveloped. With his new home now under construction, one day Edwards entered Brooks' Barbershop for a haircut. He was quickly recognized by the old man in the barber chair who asked, "Is it true you're building a house on that cursed and haunted lot?"

"I don't believe in any such foolishness," Edwards replied, "and I'm surprised that a grown man would even speak of such a silly thing out in public. Save that foolishness for Halloween to scare your grandchildren!"

The old man sadly shook his head. "I wouldn't dismiss it if I were you. I heard the lynching story straight from one of the men who were there that night. All I can tell you, sir, is that tragedy after tragedy has occurred to anyone associated with that property. Personally, I wouldn't go near it, let alone build a home there." Nothing further was said by either man as barber Matthew Brooks continued to cut his customer's hair in silence. He too thought that the events that later transpired were nothing more than coincidence and silly superstition.

Finally, to break the silence in the room, Brooks said, "Every town has its own haunted house or ghost story. But I feel the less said about that old lynching, the better off our community will be."

CHAPTER 8

The House is Completed

Foreground vacant lot & new Edwards's home
Olive and Roland Edwards Sr.

The Curse of the Hanging Tree

The Edwards were very excited to finally move into their beautiful new home. Roland had always promised his wife that when he finally made good, the couple would build their dream home. Their old house on the south side of Gas City had served them well, having raised a son, Roland Jr., there before he left for college and started his own life elsewhere. Mr. Edwards had managed to avoid the financial losses that many of his friends and associates had experienced, as he avoided investing in the risky stock market altogether. It also helped to come from a well-to-do family too, like his father; Dr. Alexander Edwards had been a successful physician for many years in Kokomo.

Despite his stern appearance, Roland was a happy-go-lucky man who enjoyed life, a good occasional cigar, and a glass of after-dinner brandy. He was a great joke teller at public gatherings. One story, in particular, he often told was about himself as a nine-year-old boy. "One day after the Sunday church sermon ended, the preacher announced he was requiring all boys and girls under the age of sixteen to memorize a passage in the Bible for next Sunday. 'When I call upon each of you,' he instructed, 'please stand and recite your chosen verse. Make sure you speak loud enough for the congregation to hear you clearly.'

"That week I worried that I would experience stage fright and forget the long passage my father had chosen for me. Try as I might, I was unable to recite the passage without my body shaking and my mind going completely blank.

"The day arrived all too soon and I tried to play sick, but my father could easily see through my masquerade, and forced me to dress for church. I remember sitting there on that hard pew waiting as name after name was called upon for recital. Each student performed admirably. Suddenly, my name was called out and I froze in place. My father nudged me to stand up and recite the Bible passage. My legs were shaking and I could see everyone looking, waiting for me to start. I panicked and uttered, 'Do not eat the yellow snow,' and dropped back into my seat. You could have heard a pin drop as the church became so quiet until someone in the back started laughing. The dirty looks he received shut him up abruptly. Our preacher's face turned deep red, but he said nothing as he called upon the remaining children. You can imagine the terrible embarrassment I inflicted upon my parents and the spanking I received when we returned home. Still, you gotta admit, it was mighty sound advice!" Yes, Rolland Edwards Sr. was a well-liked member of the business community in Gas City.

Olive Edwards had met her husband in grade school and frankly, couldn't stand him. But as each matured, she saw a different side of his personality and came to understand his playfulness. After graduation from high school, the pair became a couple and soon married. Olive liked and felt accepted by his parents and Roland seemed fond of her widowed mother. After Roland Jr. arrived, life became quite busy for the young mother. As the boy aged, she could see that in all respect, he was indeed his father's son. The years passed by all too quickly. After graduating from college, Roland Jr. moved to Muncie and became a successful businessman in his own right. There, he met and married a young woman by the name of Violet Goins.

* * * * * * * * *

One day in the spring of '97, a freak accident occurred that would forever change the lives of the Edwards family. Roland Sr. was passing through Main Street rather briskly when suddenly the right front wheel of his open-top carriage came off. His vehicle's axle dropped abruptly onto the paved street and snagged one of the bricks, twisting the carriage to its side and throwing the businessman out on the new concrete sidewalk's curb. He was transported to the doctor's office by helpful townspeople, but, unfortunately, there was little that 19th-century medical science could offer other than something to help with the pain, as the hard impact had fractured his right hip. In time, Roland Edwards came to realize he was destined to spend his days confined to a wheelchair at home. Their den was converted into a downstairs bedroom and Olive Edwards became a full-time nurse for her husband. Their visiting son and daughter-in-law were unable to help brighten the injured man's mood. "I tried to talk business with father, but he just didn't seem at all interested," he privately said to his mother.

"I know, son. I've even asked his friends and business acquaintance to visit him, but your father just won't allow himself to become mentally active again. He's telling everyone he's a victim of that silly curse and that it is dangerous to even be near him. I'm at my wit's end with worry." All young Roland could do was hug his mother as she cried.

"Father has always been strong. Let's give him time to adjust to his new situation. Maybe he'll snap out of it if." That afternoon, he and Violet returned home by train to Muncie.

The days soon turned to weeks and Olive was nearing her breaking point. It was like living with a stranger as he rarely spoke, despite her best effort at remaining positive around him. She looked forward to simply getting out of the house to obtain groceries, visit with friends, or go to church, as it gave her an all-too-brief reprieve. Roland soon began acting quite strangely, saying he heard the sounds of Indian chanting and war drums at night outside his temporary bedroom. Olive feared her husband was losing his mind. She read the Bible at every opportunity, hoping its holy message would give her the strength and comfort she so desperately needed. Even their pastor's visits seemed to have no effect in uplifting the spirits of Roland.

A few weeks later, Sunday arrived and Olive began preparing herself for church. "I'll be home as quick as I can and start lunch. Is there anything you need before I go?" She was met by silence as he sat motionless in his wheelchair staring out the living room window. The brief time she had away at church seemed like a lifesaver to her. People often came up to her and inquired about Roland's health, but she could only shake her head in sadness. There were simply no easy answers to give.

* * * * * * * * *

"I'm home," she announced after entering the unlocked front door. Looking about, she did not notice her husband as she climbed the stairs to change clothing. Returning to the first floor, she proceeded towards the kitchen, wondering what she could prepare for lunch. "Honey, did you hear me, I'm home. Where are..." Violet halted as she saw that the door leading to the basement was standing open. *That's strange*, she thought as she approached to shut it. Just as she started to swing the door, an image caught her eye causing her to stop. There at the base of the stairs, lay the crumpled wheelchair and the body of her husband. Violet screamed and rushed down the stairs to find him quite dead.

CHAPTER 9

Justin is Notified

Gas City Marshal Justin Blake 		Mrs. Virginia Blake

Justin Blake and his wife Virginia had just sat down for lunch when their new telephone rang. It was Deputy Michael Davidson. "Sorry to bother you on a Sunday, Justin, but you might want to come over here at the Roland Edwards home. Mr. Edwards is dead and things just don't look right to me."

"I'm on my way," he replied and then quickly hung up the heavy receiver. Virginia was by now quite used to her husband being called out at all hours of the day and night.

"I'll keep your lunch warm on the stove," she said.

Justin returned to their bedroom to change into his uniform. "I'll be back as quickly as I can."

* * * * * * * * *

Justin arrived and was met at the door by Deputy Davidson. "Mrs. Edwards is in the kitchen with one of her friends," he said. "Doctor Baxter just arrived and is in the basement with the body."

Doctor Horace Baxter

Doris Davidson and Deputy Michael Davidson

Justin followed Michael into a hallway, and then entered the steps leading into the large, deep basement. The partially-crumpled wheelchair had been moved to the side and out of the way. Baxter stood up as both men approached. "The neck is broken. I would venture to say he died from hard contact during the fall," he offered.

"How long would you say he's been dead, Doc?"

"Not long, Marshal. No more than a couple of hours, I would guess. I'll know more after I have the body back at my office for examination."

Justin nodded and Doctor Baxter left to make the arrangements. Davidson spoke up, "I was in the office when I got the call from Mrs. Edwards. She was so hysterical I had a hard time understanding her, then I called Doc. Justin; this just doesn't seem like an accident to me. Why would a man in a wheelchair be anywhere near an open doorway leading to the basement?"

"Have you spoken with Mrs. Edwards yet?"

"No. I thought you would want to do that. Besides, there are two ladies with her now."

Justin nodded in agreement. Looking about, he found an oil lamp sitting on a wall shelf and lit it. "Now we can see," he said. Taking the lamp in hand, Justin climbed the stairs and spent some time looking at the door and the entryway, before proceeding back down the stairs. "There doesn't appear to be anything that he might have been after. No shelf to house anything he could have been reaching for, lost his balance, and fell." Justin then approached the basement entry door leading to the outside. It was bolted shut from the inside. He then checked the windows and found them locked as well. "As of now I only see three possibilities. Either Mr. Edwards attempted suicide or, an assailant gained entry after she had left or..."

"She deliberately pushed him," Michael added.

"I need to speak with Mrs. Edwards," Justin said. "You take the other two ladies into another room and see what you can learn from them. Ask if the Edwards's were having marital troubles or if there were reports of fighting." After Michael explained why, the ladies left the side of their friend and followed him into another room.

Justin entered the kitchen to see the widow sitting at the kitchen table holding a cup of coffee, staring off blindly into space. "Mrs. Edwards, I'm not sure if you know me or not, but I'm Marshal Blake. I'm sorry but I must ask you a few questions."

"I...understand, sir," she murmured.

"Please tell me what happened here today."

"Well...I dressed for church and told Roland I was leaving. When I returned, I changed out of my good dress and started towards the kitchen to prepare our lunch. I called out to my husband to let him know I was back..but he didn't answer me. That's when I saw..." She stopped speaking and took a sip of her drink. Justin noticed that her hands were shaking.

"Your husband was confined to a wheelchair. Is that correct? Could he stand at all?"

"No, Marshal. His hip bone was broken in a carriage accident several months ago. I'm surprised you hadn't heard about it."

"I am familiar with it, ma'am, but I must ask these questions. When did you last see your husband alive?"

"It was like I said, sir, just before I left for church. He was sitting in his wheelchair looking out the living room window."

"What was his mood like recently? Have you had quarrels or problems?"

"The accident changed my husband into a shell of his former self. He rarely spoke and showed no interest in anything. And no, we haven't fought. It takes two people to fight. Because of this horrible accident, I went from being his wife to his full-time caregiver."

Justin sensed some bitterness in her statement. "So, you resented the new roll that had been forced upon you."

She looked at him with puzzlement. "I know your lovely wife, Marshal. Can you honestly tell me that if her active life was snuffed out in an incident, you wouldn't resent what life had dealt you? My husband's accident was not his fault, so no, I never blamed him, just the terrible fate that had destroyed his life and, in a way, mine also." She paused and took another sip. "I'm very sorry, sir, may I offer you a cup of coffee? I'm not being a very good hostess."

Justin ignored the offer and changed the subject. "What about his friends. Has he had recent visitors or anyone who might hold a grudge against him? Did he have any enemies?"

She shook her head. "Roland was the type who befriended everyone...until all this happened. Since then, he's shown no interest in being around anyone, even our son, or me."

"Where does your son live?"

"He and his wife live in Muncie."

"Can you think of any reason your husband might have had for trying to enter the basement? What about heating or plumbing problems?" She only shook her head.

Justin paused before continuing. "What about the possibility of suicide. Was your husband the type..."

"NO," she shouted while striking her fist hard against the tabletop. "Don't even go there, Marshal!"

Justin was slightly taken back by her sudden anger. If she had pushed her husband down those steps to his death, her saying he was indeed suicidal would have provided Mrs. Edwards with an easy alibi.

"Were both your entry doors locked when you left for church this morning?"

"We leave the doors unlocked once we're up and around. Same as most people do. We've never had any trouble with..."

Justin cut her off. "Thank you, Mrs. Edwards. Please don't leave town without checking with me first, as I may have additional questions to ask."

"I'm not going anywhere Marshal; I plan to continue living and eventually dying here in my house." Justin thanked her for her time and met up with Michael on the front porch.

"I didn't learn anything," Michael said. "No rumors of fighting or any problems. The ladies all said she was a loving wife who was determined to care for her husband all by herself. They possess the wealth to hire someone to help, but Mrs. Edwards refused to consider it. While I was waiting on you, I checked both doors and all the windows. The rear door was unlocked. There was no sign of any forcible entry." Justin thanked him.

"Check the ground for any footprints, though as dry as it's been, you probably won't see anything. Then ask the neighbors if they saw anyone lurking about this morning. I'm going home now." Justin's mind was actively searching for an answer.

If Edwards didn't commit suicide and if she didn't push him down those stairs, then what happened? Did an unknown party enter the home after she had left? I cannot make any arrests on mere suspicion. My instincts tell me she's telling the truth.

* * * * * * * * *

Justin returned home with more questions than answers. Virginia was the type of wife who seldom questioned her husband about any ongoing police business. For that, Justin was very grateful. As for his warmed-over dinner, it still tasted mighty good going down.

CHAPTER 10

The Investigation Continues

Deputy Marshal Wilbert Vance
Wife Rachael, & Mary Louise

The following morning, Deputy Marshal Wilbert Vance was soon brought up to speed on the death of Roland Edwards Sr. "Here's Doctor Baxter's medical report," Justin said. "Edwards had been dead for about two to three hours before we were notified. The body showed the normal cuts and bruises one would expect from a fall down the basement stairs. There was also a major blow to the back of the skull. That's the injury that concerns me the most. Michael checked with the neighbors, but nobody saw anyone in their neighborhood that didn't belong. If Mrs. Edwards didn't murder her husband, the assailant could have gotten entry through either unlocked door. There were no signs of forced entry, and the outside basement door was bolted from the inside."

Wilbert said, "I remember responding to his carriage accident and I heard he was confined to a wheelchair. So, what are your thoughts? Did he kill himself or did his wife or someone else murder him and try to make it look like a suicide? I wonder if they were having marital troubles? Was there any blood on her dress or, for that matter, could she have changed before your arrival?"

"Those are good questions. She was wearing a simple light-colored dress. Before I left her, I asked that she stand so I could view it and allow me to see her arms. I saw no blood. I also asked if this was the dress she was wearing when she discovered her husband's body. She said it was. We checked the laundry area and found nothing. Michael also checked her bedroom closet. Nothing was found. My instincts say she's telling us the truth, but I won't rule her out just yet. He also interviewed the ladies in another room and asked if there were family troubles they were aware of. They all claimed she was a devoted wife to him. I thought Mrs. Edward's story seemed plausible. Let's go over there now and conduct a more thorough search of the basement and living room area. One of the neighbor ladies told Michael they would be taking turns staying with her overnight, so someone should be up and let us into the house. Grab a barn lantern to take with us so we'll have better lighting to check for bloodstains in their dark basement. Maybe a second pair of eyes will notice something we missed yesterday."

"Maybe there's a fourth possible suspect we haven't mentioned. Perhaps it's that ghostly haunt that folks claim is attached to their land." Justin only shook his head at his friend's attempt at humor. "Grab your hat and let's go."

After arriving at the home, the lawmen were ushered inside by one of the neighbor ladies. "Olive finally went to sleep a few hours ago, Marshal. I hope you won't be needing to wake her up," she said.

"No, not at this time," Justin replied. "We'll be as quiet as possible. By the way, is there any word yet as to when her son will arrive?"

"Yes. He and his wife are due to arrive by train this afternoon. The funeral is scheduled for tomorrow afternoon at two o'clock." With that, she left the men to their tasks.

Justin led the way to the small hallway and opened the basement door. "Mrs. Edwards says she found this door to the basement standing wide open." Justin pulled out a match from his vest pocket, lit the barn lantern, and handed it to Wilbert. "Start at the entryway and search downward. Once you're finished go ahead and give the basement a quick going over. I'll make my way back towards the living room." Once Wilbert entered the stairway, Justin got down on his knees and searched the lower walls, baseboards, and floor for any signs of blood in the hallway. Finding nothing, he slowly made his way towards the living room. There he found what appeared to be a smeared speck of blood. *Someone must have stepped in it*, he thought. Justin continued onward and without finding anything else, proceeded towards one of the three large windows. *Mrs. Edwards said she last saw her husband alive sitting in front of a window in here but didn't say which one.* Still moving on his knees, Justin approached the first window near the ground while working upwards, searching the wall area, glass pane, and the opened dark curtains. He found nothing, then proceeded toward the second. Again, nothing was found. The third window paid off. There, halfway up, was a horizontal splattering of darkened blood on the glass pane and spreading on the edge of the curtain. *That settles it! Edwards was struck violently from behind with an object as he sat here. Then, his assailant pushed his wheelchair into the hallway, opened the basement door, and pushed him down the stairs to make it appear he committed suicide.*

Justin heard his friend approaching and turned. Wilbert was holding a metal pipe. "I discovered this laying in the shadows underneath a large wall shelf of paint cans. I can see how Michael hadn't noticed it. There appears to be blood on one end. I also noticed a couple of droplets of blood on two of the wooden steps." Justin was elated with their discoveries.

"Very good. We now know Mr. Edwards was murdered," as he pointed toward the blood splattering. "The assailant struck him as he was sitting here, either killing him outright or severely injuring him, then pushed his wheelchair down the stairs. Then the assailant threw the pipe inside the basement and it rolled under where you found it," Justin said. "I want you to take the pipe over to Doctor Baxters and ask him to verify it's human blood. I'll remain until she wakes up so I can search more thoroughly."

Then a woman's voice spoke from the edge of the room. "That won't be necessary, Marshal. I give you complete authority to search every square inch of our home. I have nothing to hide." It was the widow, Olive Edwards. She then proceeded toward a small desk and extracted a large book from a drawer. It was the family's Bible. She placed her hand upon it, saying, "I swear before Almighty God that I know nothing about my husband's murder." She then kissed its cover and placed it on top of the desk. "Ask me any questions you want, Marshal, and then find the person who murdered my beloved husband!"

"Thank you, Mrs. Edwards, for your cooperation," Justin said. "Wilbert, after you see Doc come back here and assist in the search." With the assumed murder weapon in hand, Wilbert departed.

"While you await your friend's return, how about joining me for that cup of coffee, Marshal?"

Justin smiled and followed her back into the kitchen. They then sat down at a small kitchen table. "My son Roland Jr. and his lovely wife Violet will arrive this afternoon. I would like for you to meet him," she said. After their second cup, Wilbert returned. All areas of the home were searched as well as the dress closets. No traces of blood on any clothing were found. The basket of soiled clothing was also inspected thoroughly without offering any results. Even the contents of the outside privy's hole were examined using a large tree branch, illuminated by the barn lantern. This was an unpleasant, but necessary, thing to do. Now satisfied that nothing more could be accomplished, Justin thanked Mrs. Edwards again for her cooperation.

Just before the men departed, Wilbert asked, "Mrs. Edwards, have you thought of anyone else who might have had cause to wish your husband ill will, or of anything he said recently that now strikes you as odd?"

The woman seemed to hesitate before answering. "Roland mentioned he heard strange chanting and the beating of a war drum outside the downstairs room where he slept. I know it sounds crazy, but I heard it too but didn't let on that I had. I didn't want him to become more frightened than he already appeared to be, or that he might tell one of his visiting friends. There are enough of those crazy rumors about our property going around now."

On their way back to the office Wilbert said, "Well, I guess we can rule out murder by haunt. Ghosts don't kill people using a pipe."

Justin remained quiet for a time before responding. "No, but someone pretending to be a ghost could have, and that might explain all the chanting and drum sounds. Our murderer, I can guarantee, is flesh and blood."

* * * * * * * * *

Late the following afternoon, a younger distinguished man entered the marshal's office. "I'm looking for Marshal Blake."

"I'm Blake. Can I help you?"

"Thank you, sir." He said as he took an offered seat. "I'm Roland Edwards Jr. I just came from burying my father.

I wanted to come by and find out how the search and apprehension of his killer were going, but I didn't expect to find you calmly sitting at your desk."

Justin didn't take offense to the statement, knowing it to be a very difficult time for the grieving son. "I can assure you, Mr. Edwards, we are doing all that we can at the moment. Unfortunately, there were no witnesses to your father's murder and almost no clues left. Are you aware of anyone your father may have mentioned that he had issues with before his accident?"

The young man now seemed to have his emotions better under control. "No sir. After his injury, father clammed up and spoke nothing of business and little of anything else. It was as if he had already died inside." Roland then changed the subject. "Mother told me you searched her house and belongings. Do you consider my mother a suspect, Marshal? I can swear to you that she is incapable of harming my father."

"I'm sorry, but I'm not at liberty to discuss the details of the case or whom we may or may not have ruled out."

The young man got quiet but appeared to understand. "My wife and I will be remaining in Gas City for several more days. If you decide you need to question my mother any further, I want to be present in the room." He then stood up, thanked the marshal for his time, and left. Justin sat there and considered what had been said. Unfortunately, there were no other suspects at the time, but all other possibilities would be vigorously investigated.

* * * * * * * * *

That night local Gas City tailor John Martin returned home in a drunken condition and attempted to take the life of his sixteen-year-old daughter. With a revolver, he struck her across the head, inflicting two painful wounds. He then fired about fifteen rounds into the family's piano, completely ruining it. Once notified of the assault, Deputy Marshal Davidson spent the rest of his shift attempting to locate Martin. He was later arrested in Marion. His daughter's injuries were treated by Doctor Baxter.

Chapter 11

Life Goes On For Now

Tracy Stevenson and daughter
Elizabeth Ann

Tracy Stevenson reached inside her young daughter's closet and removed an attractive lavender dress. "Here, sweetie, put this on. You and mommy are going over to Aunt Rachael's house to visit." The little girl got very excited knowing she could see and play with her younger friend, Mary Louise Vance. Tracy was a struggling young mother who had experienced a difficult start in adulthood. A local girl, Tracy met and married Melvin Stevenson, the owner of a local photography studio in what was then referred to as Harrisburg. Unfortunately, the marriage proved to be a brief one, for as soon as she became pregnant, her husband ran off with another woman he had met. The pair soon set up a new photography studio in the town of Anderson. Tracy, now abandoned and with a child on the way, was encouraged by her friend Doris Davidson to seek legal assistance. It proved to be a wise choice.

The state of Indiana took a dim view of a husband abandoning his expectant wife for another woman. After a brief hunt to locate Mr. Stevenson, he was served with divorce and abandonment papers and instructed to appear before a Grant County judge. By then, Tracy had given birth to his daughter whom she named Elizabeth Ann. The court instructed him to provide monthly alimony and child support payments to his abandoned wife or face jail time. Realizing he had been given no choice in the matter, Melvin Stevenson agreed to abide by the terms of the settlement. Now with his income drastically reduced, his live-in girlfriend sought greener pastures elsewhere. Tracy was now a single woman once again, but continued to use her former married name for the benefit of her child. Still, there was a stigma attached by many to a divorced woman, no matter the actual cause.

Doris Davidson then assisted her friend in obtaining a cheaper apartment for her and the baby to dwell in. Time passed and once Rachael Marley married Deputy Wilbert Vance, Tracy became friends with Rachael as well as Justin Blake's wife, Virginia. In striving to obtain a little extra income, Tracy provided occasional babysitting services for families requiring a few hours away.

Holding her daughter's hand, Tracy and Elizabeth made their way downstairs and out into the sunlight. The sky appeared to be darkening to the north as they made their way down the new concrete sidewalk and turned south onto Third Street. Tracy's eyes became fixed upon the luxurious Mississinewa Hotel and noticed a visiting couple entering with their suitcases. *I heard their restaurant is wonderful,* she thought. *Maybe someday I can go there and try it for myself.* They walked two more blocks before turning onto the street where her friend Rachael Vance lived. Approaching the front door, Tracy knocked and was welcomed inside. "Hey girls, come on in," a smiling Rachael Vance said. "My, that's a beautiful dress you are wearing, Elizabeth," she said to the little girl.

"Thank you," the child managed to say before running toward Mary Louise's bedroom, looking for her playmate.

"Hello, Doris," Tracy offered as she entered the living room and seated herself next to her friend. "It looks like rains coming in from the north."

Doris responded, "I hate to hear that. Michael and I were planning on a short picnic in the park once he's up and around."

"I don't know how you two ever see each other with him working nights and you working part-time at the emporium," Tracy said.

"We manage somehow, but at times it seems we are just two ships passing through the night," she joked. "At least he seems to prefer his job as a deputy rather than working in some hot, miserable factory for twelve hours. By the way, Rachael, where is your husband?"

She chuckled. "He and Justin decided to get away and to do a little fishing down at the river. The lack of evidence in that investigation of the murdered man has got them both pretty upset. I can always tell because Wilbert gets quiet and seems to stare off into space. I suggested he needed to put it all to the side for a while and to make Justin go fishing with him."

"I heard old man Edwards committed suicide, him being trapped in a wheelchair and all. Poor thing. Folks say the Edward house is built on cursed land," Tracy said. "I heard that many people suffered terribly just by being associated with it."

Rachael chimed in. "I've heard those stories too! You don't suppose...?" All three ladies laughed at the very idea of a silly curse and changed the subject.

Chapter 12

The Bet

It was a full moon night as three teenage boys made their way along the dirt street. One of them had been successful in obtaining a flask of whiskey from an unscrupulous source and was passing the bottle among the group. It didn't take long before the youths felt the effects. "There's the Edwards house," the one named Billy said. "My dad told me that the empty lot next to it was where the hanging tree once stood. That place is haunted by some Indian kid!"

The other two boys laughed at their friend's statement. "I'm not afraid of no Indian ghost," the boy named Wally said. "That's all a bunch of hooey!"

Now feeling quite brave from the effects of the whiskey, Billy replied, "Then I dare you to go sit in that empty lot all by yourself until daylight. That is...unless you're chicken!"

Wally knew he now had no way of backing out and saving face. "I'm not chicken, but why should I? And what's in it for me? What's to prevent you two from sneaking up on me in the darkness anyway?"

Billy now felt empowered. "We won't and I'll lay a fifty-cent bet on the deal too. If we try to scare you, I'll fork over the money. Bruce and I will go straight home, but how do we know you'll hold up your end of the bet?"

Come back here at daylight tomorrow morning and see for yourselves. If I'm not there on that empty lot, I'll pay each of you fifty cents!" He said it knowing full well he had no coins in his pocket. "I'll meet up with you two here tomorrow morning to collect my money," he said. "Go home now and leave me be!" The other boys laughed and made their way home.

Wally walked over to the vacant lot and sat himself down. *This was a crazy bet*, he told himself. *but I can sure use the money.* Time seemed to go slowly as he sat there looking up at the moon and the stars. Another hour passed and Wally was feeling sleepy from the alcohol. Then, he thought he heard something, the faint sound of chanting somewhere behind him. "Those two guys are trying to sneak up and scare me! I'm gonna win my bet now for sure!"

* * * * * * * * *

The two friends met up at daybreak and proceeded towards the vacant lot. "Think he stayed all night?" Bruce asked. "He could have left right after us, and then got up early."

Billy agreed. "If that's the case, we won't pay him a red cent!" Soon the youths arrived at the empty lot to find their friend was not there. "See, I told you he wouldn't be here," Billy said. "But let's check the entire property just to make sure. He might later claim he was here, but we didn't see him. You go out back and I'll go down the road. We'll meet up on the other side of the house with the picket fence."

Billy walked past the Edwards house and noticed something lying along the road, up against the picket fence. He saw it was their friend Wally. "Quit your play-acting, I see ya!"

It was then that he saw something that would forever haunt his dreams. There, beside the back of Wally's bloody skull, in a pool of dark blood, lay an Indian tomahawk.

Chapter 13

The Scene of the Crime

Location of the latest murder, outside of the fenced area.
Edwards's house is behind a large tree.

A curious crowd of locals assembled near the murder scene in an attempt to learn what had happened. By the time Marshal Blake and Deputy Vance arrived, Doctor Baxter was already present and examining the body of the young man. Seeing the tomahawk, Justin directed Wilbert to take possession of the murder weapon. The victim's friends, Billy and Bruce stood next to an older woman who was crying. She was the grandmother of the murdered boy. Justin instructed Wilber to speak with the doctor while he tried to discover what had happened. Seeing his uniform, one of the boys stepped forward and started speaking. "Marshal, our friend Wally Taylor is dead! Somebody killed him! We had a bet you see, and Wally stayed all night and..."

"Now hold on, young man. Let's start at the beginning, shall we? What are your names and addresses?" Bruce took a deep breath and started again from the beginning. Occasionally Billy jumped into the story to clarify a point "There was a tomahawk lying next to your friend's body. I know you both saw it. Does it belong to either of you?" Both boys said no. "Have either of you ever seen it before?" The response was the same. Once Justin felt he could learn no more, he approached the older woman. "Excuse me, ma'am, are you related to the victim?"

"Yes, sir, I am his grandmother. Wally came to live with me after my daughter ran off with some worthless man. I say he lives with me, but he kinda comes and goes at all hours of the day and night. Who could have done such a horrible thing to him, sir? He was a good boy. Oh, he had his faults you understand, but..."

"What was his full name, ma'am, and where do you folks live?"

"Walter Taylor. People just called him Wally, and like I said he lives with me at 221 South West D Street," she said as she regained her composure.

"Did your grandson own a tomahawk?" She replied that he did not. Justin thanked her and approached Wilbert.

"Doc says he's been dead for about six hours. That would have the time of death roughly around one-thirty this morning. The back of his head was crushed inward. Here is the presumed murder weapon," he said holding it out for Justin to inspect. "I doubt the boy knew what hit him. Have you learned why he was out here that time of night? Are you thinking those boys are responsible?" Justin said he didn't know but was going to go check with their families about their whereabouts the night before.

"They claim they made a bet that he wouldn't stay on that vacant lot all night. More of that silly ghost business, I'm afraid. Tell Doc I'll get with him later. Make a thorough search of the area for any clues that might have been left by the killer. Then go door to door and see if anyone saw or heard anything unusual last night. Maybe we'll get lucky. I'll drop off the tomahawk in the office, then go speak with the families of the boys," Justin said. After returning to his office, the bloody tomahawk was wrapped in an old newspaper and placed inside his desk drawer. He then proceeded to the first boy's home. He learned their son was home before ten o'clock. The second household produced the same information. Both also confirmed neither boy owned a tomahawk.

Wilbert returned to the office by mid-morning and went straight to the coffee pot. It was empty. "I'm sorry," Justin said, as he stood up to refill the pot. Wilbert said not to bother with it anyway and seated himself. Justin asked, "So, did you find out anything from the neighbors?"

Wilbert had a troubled look on his face. "Well, yes and no. The only people who would admit to hearing something late last night live in the house behind the fence where the body was discovered."

"What did they hear?" Justin asked.

"Would you believe both husband and wife swear they heard Indian chanting and war drums? They said that as soon as it starts getting dark, they lock their doors and never venture outside at night. I got the feeling a few others in the neighborhood may have heard this too, but chose not to speak with me about it."

A look of surprise appeared on Justin's face. "I think I'll make that pot of coffee after all."

Wilbert said that he couldn't see any connection between the homicide of Roland Edwards and the Taylor youth, other than both murders taking place nearby. "Maybe we should look closer at those two boys, and also some of Taylor's other classmates." Justin nodded in agreement.

"We still have a week of school left. Drop by and speak with the school principal. See if there's been any trouble between him and anyone else."

Later after both men finished their cup of coffee, Wilbert left to ask more questions.

* * * * * * * * *

Later that afternoon, Doctor Baxter dropped off a copy of his medical report. It stated the time of death was between one and two o'clock in the morning and that the victim died from a severe skull fracture. *That eliminates the two boys' involvement unless their parents are lying to protect them. But I think that is highly unlikely as each seemed shocked when I informed them of the murder of their son's friend. Now what?* Justin asked himself.

Soon Wilbert returned from speaking with the school authorities. There had not been any recent trouble reported involving Wally Taylor. "He seemed to have been liked by the students I spoke with," Wilbert said. "That brings us back to the chanting and drums sound. I can't help but wonder if someone, for whatever reason, is trying to keep that curse story going."

Justin had wondered the same thing. "But who would that be and what's their motive for prolonging it all these years?" Unfortunately, they had no answers.

* * * * * * * * *

A very distraught Olive Edwards sent a letter to her son Roland Jr. to inform him of the murder of the boy just one house east of her. "I'm now terrified to close my eyes at night," she wrote. Roland showed the letter to his wife Violet to get her response.

"I think we need to go to Gas City and spend a few days with her," she replied.

"I think you are right," he said. The next morning, with suitcases and a long tube in hand, Roland and Violet Edwards boarded the northbound train to Gas City. He planned to encourage his mother to sell out and move to Muncie so he and Violet could properly care for her. If that idea didn't succeed, he had a second suggestion he would make.

CHAPTER 14

A Decision was Made

Once in town, a small carriage was rented from the nearby livery stable and the couple proceeded to his mother's home. They were met at the door by an overjoyed Olive Edwards. "I am so thrilled you both are here," she said as tears streamed down both cheeks. After hugging his mother, Roland carried their luggage upstairs while Violet accompanied her mother-in-law into the living room. "You both must think I'm a silly old woman," she exclaimed while wiping her moist eyes with a handkerchief. "I don't want to keep bothering either of you. I know Roland's business keeps him very busy."

"Not at all, Mother," Violet replied. "Roland doesn't go to an office every day as other men do. He can manage his investments whenever the need arises. So please, don't feel you're putting us out. You're not."

Roland soon entered the room and seated himself next to his wife on the couch. After a bit of normal chatter, he got right to the point. "Mother, Violet and I have talked and we feel it would be best for you to sell this house and move in with us in Muncie." He then looked about the room before returning his sight to his mother. "Besides, this place holds bad memories for you. You need to get away from it."

Mother Edwards seemed prepared with her answer. "Son, this is my home. Yes, your father's murder holds bad memories for me here, but there are plenty of good ones too. Thank you for your offer, but no. I wish to remain here for the rest of my life. And besides," she joked, "remember the old phrase about too many cooks in the kitchen."

Violet immediately responded. "Mother, I would welcome your cooking expertise. I'm embarrassed to admit I am a terrible cook, and as a result, we eat out a lot of the time."

Mother Edwards smiled over at her daughter-in-law. "Thank you, dear, but I prefer to remain here."

Seeing that they were unable to persuade her, Roland reverted to Plan B. "Then how about selling me that empty lot beside you so we can build ourselves a new home and move here? I've brought with me a complete set of architectural drawings for a lovely home Violet and I have toured in Muncie. How much do you want for your lot?"

Elation appeared upon the face of Mother Edwards before caution returned. "But what about your business in Muncie? How would you manage?"

"When I need to return in person, I'll just catch the train back there. Otherwise, there won't be any problem that I can't work out by sending a telegram to my investment companies."

"Son, it just wouldn't be fair for me to ask you to uproot your lives and move here, just for my benefit."

This time it was Violet who responded by reaching for her mother-in-law's hand. "Mother, we love you and want to be near you! Besides...I was getting a little bored with Muncie anyway!"

Roland quickly replied, "So what is your asking price for the vacant lot?"

The older woman smiled. "You can have it for the price of a silver dollar."

"Done! I'll locate one of the town's lawyers and get it all drawn up. Mother, you are going to love our new home. One of our dearest friends had it built and we fell in love with its layout. He was gracious enough to give me their construction plans, which I brought along today. As soon as the land transfer is complete, I'll hire the best contractor around. Hopefully, we can be living here by fall."

Olive Edwards was thrilled. Soon though, a more unpleasant topic was brought up. "Has your lame marshal made any progress in solving father's murder?"

The happy smile left his mother's face. "Nothing that I have heard. He even suspected me for a brief time, I hear, and I still get an occasional harsh look from people I meet on the street."

"Anger appeared upon Roland's face. "That's crazy. I will be visiting his office tomorrow and see what's being done." The subject changed and Mother Edwards slept soundly that night with the knowledge that her prayers have been answered.

* * * * * * * * *

The following morning, Justin and Wilbert arrived to relieve Michael Davidson. "Have a quiet night?" Justin asked his deputy.

"Pretty much so. I did have to break up a fight between Joe Faith and his brother in front of Rothchild's bowling alley. But other than that, it was pretty quiet. Anything new on the two homicides?" Before Justin could answer, Michael continued. "Doris is starting to believe all that curse nonsense, but I'm wondering if someone wants us to think along those lines." He gave a short wave and left for home.

"It sounds like we're all thinking the same thing," Wilbert said.

* * * * * * * * *

After completing a quick claim deed for the new property, Roland Edwards Jr. asked about hiring a dependable contractor and soon spoke with the suggested man. An agreement was reached after the architectural drawings had been reviewed. "I see no major issues in having your new home finished by late September or early October, Mr. Edwards, that is unless the weather becomes an issue," the contractor said. "I'll certainly keep you informed by telegram as to our progress."

"I plan on returning here every few weeks anyway," Roland said. "If you need me, I'll drop everything and come." Now that their new home project had been set into motion, it was time to pay another visit with Marshal Justin Blake.

* * * * * * * * *

Justin recognized his new visitor as soon as he entered their office. "Hello, Mr. Edwards. Please have a seat."

"Marshal, I see you remember me. My wife and I are in town to visit with my mother and to tend to some business; I wanted to stop in and see how your investigation on my father's murder was progressing."

Justin wished he had better news. "We seem to have hit a dead-end. There were no clues left at the scene of the crime, no witnesses, or even a possible motive. The case, unfortunately, remains open. I realize this is not what you wanted to hear, but I have not given up hope in bringing the assailant to justice."

Roland sat staring at the marshal for several seconds before saying, "I have also heard a young boy was murdered close to mother's property. Do you think both murders are somehow connected?"

"At this point, we are keeping all our options open."

"I see," Roland said. "My wife and I are going to build a house next to mother's so that we can help and protect her. I'll be returning from Muncie from time to time to check on its progress. I'll be in touch, sir." He then stood and left the office.

Justin could completely understand the man's impatience with the lack of progress, as he too felt the same way.

* * * * * * * * *

Summer was slowly passing by and the new Edwards home was nearing its completion. Mother Edwards had taken an early interest in the project, roaming about asking questions and generally being a mild nuisance. She became a familiar sight to the tradesmen going about their work. Finally, towards early August, the house was completed and ready for the family's household furniture to be shipped by rail to Gas City. Mother Edwards worked with a group of men to unload the railcar once it arrived and to deliver everything to the house. She found great enjoyment in arranging the furniture as she thought best. Roland and Violet were away on a short vacation to Chicago and would soon arrive at their new permanent home. Mother Edwards could not be happier.

CHAPTER 15

A New Beginning

The new Edwards estate,
East North C Street

Mrs. Violet Edwards,
and husband Roland Jr.

New domestic servant,
Miss Sandra Lawrence

The Curse of the Hanging Tree

It had been a busy time for new homeowners Roland Jr. and his wife Violet since returning from Chicago. There was much that needed to be unboxed and organized, and Violet wished to rearrange a few pieces of furniture from her mother-in-law's selected locations. Still, things were beginning to fall into place. Roland was meeting other businessmen and he felt that Gas City had a solid future. He soon attended a city council meeting and, afterward, introduced himself to Mayor Davis Huffman and members of the city council.

Violet planned for a housewarming party the following week, hoping to meet other wives and become an accepted member of local society. She considered herself an able housekeeper, but for whatever reason, had failed to learn the art of cooking from her mother. Then one day, that problem appeared to be solved when Sandra Lawrence appeared at their door looking for employment, stressing her gourmet abilities. She was hired on a week's trial period and remained afterward; however, there was something different about their new cook. She spoke very little and was quite vague as to her personal local history. Violet finally gave up trying to befriend the woman and let her be. Sandra was soon provided with a small upstairs guest bedroom. Other than going out to obtain needed groceries, she seldom left the property. When she did venture out in the evenings, it was to sit alone in a chair on the back porch. She declined repeated offers to accompany the couple to church on Sundays.

* * * * * * * * *

The day of the housewarming party soon arrived. Sandra had prepared a large ham that was sliced thin for sandwiches and other snacks for their expected guests. People they had met in church, as well as many new friends of Roland, along with their wives, slowly began appearing. Violet mingled with her assembled guests and ensured they had plenty to eat. Mother Edwards was on hand and had requested some of her friends to drop by also. Violet was very pleased with the turnout and found herself invited into the private circle of Gas City society. As she mingled about, an older man approached and asked, "Mrs. Edwards, are you aware of the horrid history of your property? People say it's haunted, you know."

Mother Edwards heard the statement and attempted to downplay it. "Pay no attention to that silly old wives' tale, my dear. It's just gossip."

The man realized it best not to challenge Mother Edwards's statement, returning instead to the table for another plate of small sandwiches. Now very curious about what the man said, Violet Edwards made a mental note to investigate this strange story further.

* * * * * * * * *

The following Monday while Violet was shopping in a lady's hat shop, she bumped into one of her female guests. "Let me see now," she said, trying to recall her name. "It's Doris, right?" The lady was Doris Davidson, the wife of night deputy marshal Michael Davidson.

"You remembered," she replied, pleased to have made a good impression. "That was a lovely party you hosted, Violet. I am sorry that my husband Michael couldn't attend, but he is a deputy marshal and works all kinds of strange hours. I was curious if the bonnet I have been admiring in the shop's window was still here, but apparently, it's been sold. Oh well, a day late and a dollar short I always say!" she joked.

"Doris, let me ask you about something I heard that evening. Do you know anything about our property supposedly being haunted?" she chuckled.

Doris smiled. "Why don't we go over to the diner and have a cup of coffee and I'll tell you what I've heard. I don't know that I believe it or not, but it's an interesting story and we can get caught up on other matters too." The ladies left the hat shop and crossed the street to the small diner. Once seated and their drinks ordered, Doris began. "From what I've heard, long ago an innocent boy was lynched…"

That evening Violet repeated the story to her husband, who only laughed and shook his head. "I'm sorry dear, but I just don't believe in curses, spooks, or ghostly goblins. It's all just coincidences that those things happened anyway." Nothing further was said and he considered the subject closed. Other events would soon prove otherwise.

* * * * * * * *

A few days later Roland appeared at his mother's home to try to fix a leak in the kitchen sink's waterline. He had his head and shoulders shoved underneath the kitchen cabinet as his mother sat nearby at the small kitchen table watching. They had been making light conversation as he struggled with the piping. "I hate plumbing," he exclaimed with disgust in his voice. Realizing he should not have complained out loud about the task, he decided to lighten the subject. "Mother,

Violet told me the strangest story about a supposed curse on our property. Have you ever heard anything like that? I had a difficult time not laughing in her face."

The mood in the room suddenly changed. "I'm sorry that man brought it up at your party. I was hoping Violet would never hear about it and start to worry. Yes, son, I know all about it. While I was never an actual believer, I can tell you now that your father eventually came around to thinking it might be true. We each heard and saw strange things we couldn't explain. Remember, no one ever discovered how the wheel on our carriage suddenly became loose and caused your father's terrible accident. Afterward, people began adding that with many of the other supposedly incidents happening here, starting with that lynching back in '85 and ending with that teenage boy's murder. Folks say he was slain with an Indian tomahawk. I think people are secretly hoping something will happen to me, and now to you and Violet, so they can keep the old stories going. Son, I suggest you try to put it out of your mind and not worry. Now that you are here, I feel as safe as if in your father's arms. Please try to assure Violet she has nothing to be concerned about."

Finally, Roland succeeded in fixing the leaking pipe and returned home. He decided never to speak about the silly curse thing again with Violet or anyone else, and thus, put an end to its source once and for all.

* * * * * * * * *

When the family had lived in Muncie, Roland was an active member in an organization known as the Independent

Order of Red Men. Despite its odd name, it was not made up of Indians. Here are their membership requirements:

No person shall be entitled to adoption into the Order except a free white male of good moral character and standing, of the full age of twenty-one great suns, who believes in the existence of a Great Spirit, the Creator and Preserver of the Universe, and is possessed of some known reputable means of support.

The organization traced its roots back to the 1773 group of colonists known as the Sons of Liberty in Boston, who met to protest the tax imposed by Great Britton on tea. With their protests ignored, the men dressed as Mohawk Indians and proceeded to Boston Harbor, where they threw overboard 342 chests of English tea. Thus, the phrase, "Boston Tea Party" originated.

The Gas City Tribe met every Friday evening and were pleased to welcome Roland Edwards Jr. into their fold. It was a great place for men to come together and socialize, and perhaps develop future business opportunities. That night, Roland returned home before eleven o'clock to find a terrified Violet awaiting his arrival. "I am so afraid," she told him in a trembling voice. "I was sitting in the library reading when I started hearing what sounded like strange chanting outside the window. I immediately looked about, but it was too dark to see anything. I heard it on and off again at various locations outside our house. I sat waiting, hoping to catch a glimpse of the perpetrator if the chanting continued. I soon heard the sound coming from outside the rear kitchen window, and I immediately sprang into action. That is when I saw it...a strange ghostly figure moving from the toolshed and disappearing behind the barn. Darling, I nearly fainted from fright! Oh, what have we done in moving here? The stories people are telling are true!" She began to cry. Roland took her into his arms and tried to comfort her.

"Honey, what you heard was nothing, most likely only the wind. As for the spooky figure, well, it was probably only a firefly or several of them flying close together. Yes, that has to be it. Now, try to calm yourself and everything will be just fine."

"Roland, it's too late in the season for fireflies. I'm telling you I saw something and I expect you to believe me and not brush me off, like some wild, crazy person."

He realized that he was sounding condescending. "You're right. I'm sorry. I just didn't want you to be afraid to live in your own home. There has to be some kind of logical explanation for what you saw and heard. I promise you, working together, we will find the answer. But what about Sandra? Did you ask if she saw or heard it also?"

"I never thought to ask her. As you know, after she washed up the supper dishes, she goes straight to her room for the night."

His milder tone made Violet feel better and she soon began to relax. The couple then turned in for the night, but Roland had trouble going to sleep. What he had not disclosed was that he also heard strange chanting somewhere outside one evening while she was away visiting a friend. Roland was determined not to show any concern around his wife, or his mother, but was resolved to maintain vigilance for anything out of the ordinary that might occur after dark.

CHAPTER 16

In Other News

A few days later an advertisement appeared in the Gas City Journal newspaper. It read:

> Information is sought from the general public concerning the recent murders of Roland Edwards and Wally Taylor. No speck of information is too small. Please contact the marshal's office at once.
>
> Justin Blake
> Gas City Marshal

The days passed with no new leads. Justin was feeling intense pressure from Mayor Huffman and the city council to solve these murders. As for Justin himself, he was having trouble sleeping and the stress was taking its toll on him physically. His wife Virginia suggested they take a short getaway vacation, but he refused to consider the idea. "Maybe in the spring," he told her.

Those Gas City residents taking the Marion Chronicle newspaper seemed interested to read the published story concerning a man who was recently arrested for being too lazy and abusive to his wife. The story read:

> *George Jenkins, who lives in the 1700 block on West Fourth Street, is in trouble again, and it is said he will not escape so easily this time as in the past. He is said to be about the most worthless man known to the Marion police department, and on many occasions, has been hauled before the authorities to explain why he did not work and assist in the care of his large family. Through the pleading of his wife and promises to go to work and provide for his family, Jenkins has always escaped with light punishment in the past. The officers say that now he is in trouble again, he will be shown no mercy. He is under arrest in jail.*
>
> *Mrs. Jenkins appeared at police headquarters Wednesday morning and filed an affidavit against her husband in which she charged assault and battery. She presented a badly bruised face and throat as evidence of the*

beating that her husband had administered to her.

According to the story told to the police by Mrs. Jenkins, her husband awoke at three o'clock in the morning a few days ago and at once started hostilities, which resulted in her being dragged from the bed, choked, and beaten until she had to flee the house. Since that time, she says she had been afraid to return to her home. She says she has seven children at home, the smallest of which is but two years of age, and that she has been working at the Soldier's Home and supporting these children and her husband. Mrs. Jenkins told the police that she wished to go home to her children, and would do so as soon as her husband was arrested, but that she was afraid to go while he was there.

Most readers thought he should be jailed and the key thrown away.

* * * * * * * * *

Over at Brooks' Barbershop in Gas City, the story was being openly discussed by several of his customers. Barber Matthew Brooks soon began to tire of hearing about it over and over. "I'm greatly surprised he hadn't already been paid a friendly visit by the White Caps," the man in the barber chair said. The groups known as the White Caps were a band of local men and yes, a few women, who wore white hoods over their heads and paid late-night visits to those who they deemed needing vigilante justice. Prostitutes, drunkards who failed to support their families, wife beaters, Negros, and those who the law didn't or couldn't touch were their targets. Tar and feathering and whipping were tools of their trade, and in most instances, their victims soon left town to escape any future midnight visits.

The White Caps resided secretly within many communities and states throughout the country. Their members were seldom caught, but those who were were tried by the legal system and normally punished. Still, there were times when their actions were casually overlooked by the local authorities. That was not the case in Gas City. Marshal Blake and the White Caps had a history of clashing, and their members, no matter who they were, were brought to justice.

CHAPTER 17

Thursday, November 4

Wilbert Vance considered himself a lucky man. His lovely wife Rachael never complained when her husband was suddenly switched from working days to nights. Whenever one of the night deputies had a situation requiring their absence, Wilbert's working hours were changed so that he could fill in, leaving Justin alone during the day. Occasionally, both of them worked into the night whenever a stakeout or a special circumstance required it. With the death of the father of one of the other deputies, Wilbert found himself moved once again. He also knew that this coming weekend was payday for most of the factory workers in town, and thus, the saloons would be busy. Hardworking men with cash in their pockets tended to get out of control once in a while. Fistfights, minor injuries, destruction of property, and an occasional shooting seemed to go hand-in-hand, requiring the presence of two deputies to handle. Justin allowed his friend two days off to prepare for what was expected to be a busy Friday and Saturday night.

"Have you made any plans for the nights that I'm working?" Wilbert asked Rachael.

"I'm thinking of visiting with Tracy if she's available. She's promised to teach me her family's recipe for making peanut butter cookies," she said. "If not, I guess I'll find something to keep me and little Mary Louise entertained."

"Umm, those sounds delicious! Please save a few for me and I'll have them for lunch once I wake up."

She smiled. "I sure will. Who are you working with tonight?"

"I think it's Michael."

"Good. Keep your head down and come back to me with all your front teeth," she joked. Wilbert promised he'd do his best to return that way. He kissed her goodbye and left for work.

* * * * * * * * *

Friday night was indeed a busy one. Two competing glass factory men commenced brawling in a saloon down by the river. Soon, their friends jumped in, resulting in some broken tables, chairs, and the shattering of the bar mirror. The large Irish bartender finally was able to break up the fight, having to administer some gentle persuasion with his Billy club. By the time Wilbert and Michael arrived, the situation was pretty much under control. The brawlers were placed under arrest and marched to the jail where they spent a crowded, uncomfortable night. The following morning, the group appeared before

'Squire Williamson inside the rented city room inside the First National Bank building. A list of damages was presented by the saloon owner and the men were instructed to pay for them or face thirty days in the county hoosegow. At the request of the owner, each man was also forbidden to enter his saloon for two weeks, and then only if each promised to behave. Reluctantly, the men forked over the money and the damages were settled.

The next morning after awakening from six hours of sleep, Wilbert entered the kitchen for lunch and found five peanut butter cookies awaiting his enjoyment. They were delicious. Most likely due to the events of Friday night, Saturday night proved relatively quiet.

* * * * * * * * *

Wilbert returned to the office on Monday morning as usual and filled Justin in on what happened Friday night. "I'll never understand why some grown men have to act like loud and rowdy children after consuming large quantities of alcohol," Wilbert joked. He had gotten up to pour another cup of coffee when a visitor entered the office. It was Roland Edwards Jr. Justin prepared for trouble and offered the man a chair, but was very surprised at what was uttered.

"Marshal, my mother was attacked Saturday night at her home and fell down the stairs. Thank God she wasn't severely injured other than cuts, deep bruises, and a severely sprained ankle. Luckily, she managed to halt her fall mid-way down the flight. I found her yesterday morning when I went to escort her to our carriage for church services."

Justin was alarmed. "Did she recognize her attacker, Mr. Edwards? Our office is manned around the clock, sir. Why didn't you inform my officer on duty yesterday?"

Wilbert noticed a strange look on Edward's face as he didn't reply immediately. "May I offer you a cup of coffee, sir?" he asked their visitor. Edwards shook his head.

"Well, Marshal, under the circumstances I wanted to wait and speak with you directly and give myself proper time to try to come to grips with what Mother told me. You see, she had eaten supper with us Saturday night and remained until about eight o'clock before returning home. After what happened to Father, Mother has begun locking the doors when she is away, but on Saturday, she left the back door unlocked since she would be next door anyway. She said she entered the door and proceeded through the kitchen, into the hallway, and up the stairs. She had just cleared the upper landing and was approaching her bedroom when something jumped out of the open doorway towards her. Instantly, Mom took several steps backward screaming in terror. Without realizing it, she stepped back onto the stairs and fell. Mom thought she remembered grabbing hold of a baluster, but struck her head heavily, knocking herself out. She said she finally regained consciousness sometime during the early morning hours, but due to the pain, she was unable to get up. She laid there until I used my front door key, entered, and found her. Doctor Baxter came shortly after and treated her. She is to remain in bed for a while and can only get up with assistance from either Violet or myself. We are going to take turns staying with her overnight or until she can safely get up and around by herself."

"Did she notice anything at all about her attacker? Was it a man or a woman? Height, weight, hair color? Anything might help us." Justin asked.

Edwards shook his head. "None of the above. She swears it was a ghost!"

Justin and Wilbert looked at each other. "How do you arrest a ghost?" Wilbert replied.

"What is your opinion of all of this," Mr. Edwards.

"Marshal, if you had told me a year ago what I am about to say, I would have considered you mad. My wife and I have both heard occasional strange chanting and the sound of a drum beating at night. Violet even saw a glowing mist moving about one night in our backyard. I can tell you, it scared her half to death. Mother has heard things too, and once told me Father did as well. I just don't know what to say without you thinking I'm crazy."

Justin thought for a moment before asking, "How soon can one of us interview your mother?"

"Violet is with her now," Edwards said. "But I'll let you inside whenever you want."

"Deputy Vance here will return with you now, if that is alright." It was. An hour later Wilbert returned to the office. Justin couldn't wait to hear what he had discovered.

"She's convinced she saw a ghost...a white ghost that flew out of her bedroom straight at her. I'll tell you one thing, if this story gets out, the whole town will have ghost fever."

* * * * * * * * *

It got out. Nobody could rightly pinpoint the source of the leak, but just as Wilbert had predicted, the story quickly spread all over town and into neighboring Jonesboro. Even a reporter from the Gas City Journal newspaper requested an interview with the Edward family. That request was denied.

Two days later, Mother Edwards was able to get around on her own. Roland Edwards was sitting at home in the library reading one afternoon when his attention was drawn to a knock on their front door. Opening it, he saw an older man with a white beard standing before him holding an open Bible. "Mr. Edwards? I am Brother Jacobs and I am here to help you, sir."

Chapter 18

An Offer to Help

Brother Jacobs

The man calling himself Brother Jacobs was a member of the United Society of Believers in Christ's Second Coming religious organization, commonly referred to as the Shakers. Theres' was an agricultural community where all property was shared; like the Quakers, the Shakers were pacifists and practiced simplicity in their dress, speech, and mannerisms. They didn't believe in procreation, choosing instead to adopt children and recruit converts into their community. Men and women were housed, ate, worked, and worshiped separately. The name Shakers was derived from what happened during their religious services. After silent meditation, they suddenly became 'moved by the spirit' and began to shake uncontrollably, dancing, singing, and speaking in tongues. The gift of prophecy, faith-healing, and spiritual trances were a part of their belief system.

Brother Jacobs had arrived at the Terre Haute Shaker Community as an orphaned child along with his younger brother. Upon reaching the age of twenty-one, each brother and sister were given the choice to remain within the community or to leave. His brother left and eventually settled down on a small farm in North Jonesboro. When the Terre Haute Shaker Community ended due to a lack of new members, Brother Jacobs had two choices: either to move to one of the few remaining communities in Ohio and Kentucky, or to spend his remaining years at his brother's farm. He chose the latter, but retained and practiced a lifetime of Shaker teachings.

"I have heard of your terrible plight," he told Roland Edwards. "Evil cast upon this land by a wicked sorcerous sorcerous under the control of Satan. Only the Holy Word of God, spoken loudly by his messenger, will rid this cursed land from the devil's touch. I ask nothing from you, Mr. Edwards. My reward shall be received upon my death as I stand before my Savior. I ask that you allow me to attempt to cast off the evil shackles that have permeated this land for these many years."

Roland Edwards didn't know if this strange man was serious or an escapee from Richmond Mental Hospital. "I don't know...just how would you go about cleansing this land anyway?"

"I, as His assistant, will walk over every square foot of the acreage that once lay abandoned and read out loud the Holy Word! I shall enter into your dwellings and recite His Word room by room to cast out the evil that dwells there. Please have faith in the Word, Brother Edwards! I will remain as long as it takes to restore peace upon this land. May I have your blessing to begin?"

Before Roland could respond, the visitor said, "Then it is settled. Let us begin within your mother's home," as the bearded man began walking toward her home. Now very curious, Roland followed and opened the door for their visitor. "Let us begin. I wish to speak with your mother first." As if he knew the way, the religious man started climbing the stairs and knocked upon her closed bedroom door. Mother Edwards was sitting in her rocking chair reading her Bible.

"Come in, please," came the woman's voice. She was quite startled to see this strange-looking man enter along with her son.

"Mother, may I introduce to you Brother Jacobs who thinks he might be able to help us."

The stranger saw that the seated woman was holding an open Bible in her lap. "Sister Edwards, I am delighted to meet a fellow believer in the power and glory of the good book." He then went on to explain his intentions. She quickly perked up and was able to get a few words in. She told him of her husband's murder, of hearing chanting and drums behind her home, and finally of seeing the ghost that injured her. As she spoke, he nodded his understanding.

"Sister Edwards, fear not as the Lord is with you and guides us through his Holy Word." He then started reading scripture out loud, though most of it appeared to come from memory. The brother gestured feverishly with his hands as he moved about as if to drive away unseen spirits. Finally, he moved about the other rooms doing the same. Roland followed him downstairs and he continued, shouting for evil to depart the home. Finally, he asked to be taken to the basement. When finished, the men exited the front door and stood on the porch.

Brother Edwards, said softly, "I must now rest and pray before I may continue toward your own home." He went over and sat under a tree to quietly meditate.

Roland hurried home and told Violet what had happened. "He'll be coming over here shortly. I didn't know how to tell him no as he's such a forceful man and he genuinely seems to want to help. I guess what he's doing won't hurt."

Violet had other ideas. "You shouldn't have let him near your mother! We don't know a thing about him and he might make whatever evil is present even angrier." At that point, there was a loud knock on the front door.

"He's here. I think he's harmless. Let's just let him have his way, alright?" Roland opened the door and Brother Jacobs entered.

"I am ready to cleanse your home now. After comes the difficult part of cleansing the land itself. As I've been told, the witch placed a curse upon the land and all that may dwell upon it. So, it may take a few days to complete my work. I am ready to begin here now." Violet entered the room and Brother Jacobs appeared most gracious in meeting her. He then set upon his work. Finally, he entered the kitchen and suddenly stopped cold upon seeing the cook, Sandra Lawrence. "It's you," he said with surprise in his voice. The two stared at each other for a few seconds, and then he left the room. Brother Jacobs announced he was returning home to Jonesboro for the night. "I shall return at dawn to continue the Lord's work," he informed Mr. and Mrs. Edwards. As usual, Sandra never said a word and continued her food preparation.

Bright and early the next morning, Brother Jacobs had arrived, walking the land along the road and behind the neighbor's homes. His loud preaching could be heard a block away and did not go unnoticed by the other residents of the neighborhood. That afternoon, one of the neighbor men entered Matthew Brooks' Barbershop.

"There's some kind of nut walking all around our neighborhood preaching at the top of his lungs, shouting that evil must leave forever. He must be trying to rid us of that ghost!" The story soon spread all over town.

The following morning Brother Jacobs planned to give the properties around both Edward homes a final going over, then call it quits. There were still the two barns, one gardening shed, and two outbuildings to cleanse. The two barns were covered very thoroughly with his preaching. As for the others, very little time was spent inside them. Walking toward the lone gardening shed that sat behind Mother Edwards's home, Brother Jacobs was reaching for the unlocked door when suddenly, something seemed to explode right beside his hand. The door he was about to open had a chunk missing from it, and what appeared to be a bullet hole. Someone had taken a shot at him and luckily missed.

After reporting the incident to Roland Edwards, Brother Jacobs announced he had finished and was leaving for home. "Would you mind stopping by the marshal's office and telling him about what happened?" Brother Jacobs said he would be happy to. He found both lawmen at the office and explained who he was, the service he was conducting in the name of the Lord, and about the shooting incident. After a few more questions, Justin thanked him and said they would investigate. Brother Jacobs returned to his brother's farm on Kokomo Road to continue his work, crafting custom-made wooden furniture that he sold to pay for his living expenses.

Justin and Wilbert soon arrived at the Edwards residence and examined the damage. "Small caliber, probably from a twenty-two. It makes me wonder why someone didn't want Brother Jacobs to open the door." He turned to Roland Edwards. "What have you got stored inside?"

"Only Father's gardening tools, I assume. I haven't looked inside for a long time. Mother and I hire a gardener who brings his own equipment." Edwards opened the shed door and the three began a casual search. It didn't take long until an answer was found. "That finally puts the ghost story to bed once and for all!" Roland said. Inside Wilbert had discovered a small wooden box containing a candle, a box of matches, a child's toy drum, and a white bedsheet with eye holes cut out.

"Boo!" Wilbert shouted after dawning the sheet over his head and body.

Justin didn't laugh. "We still have a very dangerous killer on our hands who, once they learn that their ghost pretense has been discovered, will have to find another means of continuing their vicious murder scheme."

* * * * * * * * *

Later that afternoon, Justin and Wilbert again hashed out everything that had happened up until the present, but a suspect continued to remain oblivious. "Everything to this point revolves around that specific area of land. The killer knows the bullet missed its target and they probably suspect we have discovered their phony ghost outfit. With only one officer on duty tonight and tomorrow night, I'm wondering if you and I should return after supper and stake out the front and rear of the property in case our murderer returns?" Justin suggested.

The thought of returning to duty until late was not appealing, but Wilbert knew there were no other possible leads to pursue and agreed to the plan. Neither of their wives seemed overjoyed but offered no resistance. After all, long hours went with a lawman's job.

After meeting at the office, both men waited until darkness set in before proceeding to their stakeout. By nearly eleven o'clock, Justin approached where Wilbert was in hiding and sent him home for the night. "Maybe tomorrow night will produce better results," he said.

CHAPTER 19

Another Stakeout is Planned

After last night's failed effort, Justin suggested another course of action. "I think we may have downplayed the shooting incident a bit. I initially assumed the shot was a warning from the assailant to keep Brother Jacobs out of the gardening shed, abandon his religious quest, and leave the property at once. Instead, he reported the shooting and involved us in the investigation and the discovery of the ghost props. Now, I wonder if the assailant considers Brother Jacobs an active participant in all this cursed land nonsense. Coming this far, I just don't see him packing up and stopping his terror streak for good. He may be watching the brother's home and workshop for an opportunity to strike again."

Wilbert considered this angle. "The old man said he lived in North Jonesboro, off of Kokomo Road at his brother's farm, which sits across from the academy schoolhouse. I have heard the Shakers work long hours from dawn to dusk, and he told us he builds furniture out in a barn. That would make him an easy target for our killer."

Justin agreed. "Other than the shooting incident, our assailant has always made his appearance after dark. Even on a farm, there is always the possibility of being seen during the day. No, I think striking after dark would seem the logical time to do so. So the question is, when?"

"You know, that parcel of land is out of our jurisdiction," Wilbert offered.

"I know. Jonesboro's marshal's office has less staffing than ours, so I doubt they could provide much assistance in the stakeout. Instead, I think I'll go see their marshal and ask if they would be willing to look the other way for us."

"Yes," Wilbert said. "And if we were successful in a capture, we would automatically give them credit for working alongside us. Let me go first tonight. I'll ride out there later and look the place over, to see exactly where he works, and draw us a map of the location with good hiding spots. Then we can trade off tomorrow."

"Good," Justin replied. "Once things settle in for the night, give it up and go home. No need to meet up here just to say that nothing happened. I'll do the same, but I hope to have better luck, and maybe you'll find the assailant safely tucked away behind bars when you come in tomorrow morning." Wilbert smiled at the thought as Justin left.

Less than half an hour later he returned. "We have their permission. Take my horse and check out the place." Wilbert grabbed a writing tablet of paper and a pencil, then departed.

Traveling west, he rode over the bridge, turned right onto the road leading north, and traveled the short distance to Kokomo Road. There, he steered the horse left and spotted the academy schoolhouse. Across from it lay the Jacobs farm. Wilbert stopped, tied off the horse, as his eyes searched over the property. On the west side sat a simple two-story farmhouse with a large Maple tree out front. To its right about a hundred feet, was the large wooden barn. It appeared to be a typical farmer's barn with windows and a wide door facing the road. The door was standing wide open. Brother Jacobs had told them that he used one of its corners for his workshop, so Wilbert crept closer and began to peer through each window until he saw the old man busy at his work. Wilbert returned to where he'd tied off Justin's horse and began to sketch everything on the property. Once finished, he returned to the office and sat the tablet down on the desk for Justin to see.

"Here is the layout. Brother Jacob's workshop is here, in the eastern corner of the barn. You can see him through this window," he said as he pointed.

"What about having adequate cover?" Justin asked.

"A few trees in the distance, but there is a horse trough right here to the right of the barn door. That's probably where I'll lay in wait until I see him dimming his lanterns to quit for the night. Then I'll move away towards this large tree until he enters the house. Too bad Jonesboro couldn't supply an additional officer to watch the house all night. Our killer might arrive at two o'clock in the morning to set fire to the house."

Justin realized this was the best they could do and was pleased with the plan. Now all they had to do was wait until evening to begin their stakeouts.

* * * * * * * * *

That evening at their supper table, Wilbert told Rachael he had another stakeout that night. "Please bundle up, dear," she told him. "We might be getting some snow by early morning."

"I should be home by midnight. Don't wait up for me." After finishing his meal, Wilbert kissed little Mary Louise and Rachael goodbye. Taking her advice, he bundled up in layers of clothing for what would be a cold, lonely night before leaving for the office to await the approach of darkness.

* * * * * * * * *

Justin planned to take turns watching the front and rear of the two Edwards properties, as well as the adjoining homes. He too had bundled up, hoping and praying that somehow the killer would be soon caught and end this reign of terror once and for all.

* * * * * * * * *

Wilbert had left their office an hour before darkness set in so he could arrive on foot near the appointed time. Once there, he could see that the barn door had been closed and light produced by lanterns was emitting from the east window. After a glance, he could see Brother Jacobs was still inside. Wilbert walked up and laid down on the ground between the horse trough and the barn. The ground was cold as he lay shivering in wait, with his trusty revolver ready to use if needed. The minutes seemed to tick by slowly. *I've got to remind Justin to bring a blanket to lay on tomorrow when it is his turn to be here,* he told himself. Another hour passed by as he watched the illumination of barn lanterns inside, and occasionally heard Brother Jacobs moving about. And then, Wilbert heard a sound behind him of movement through the grass, as someone was approaching from the way he had come. Peeking around the corner of the horse trough, he could faintly make out the figure of one person. Wilbert watched intently as the person neared. *What if it's just a friend coming to visit the brother?* That concern was quickly put to rest as the figure stopped just short of the barn, raised its arm, and started approaching the lighted window. The figure held a pistol as they silently crept forward. Wilbert already had hold of his weapon, jumped to his feet, and in a commanding voice said, "Drop your weapon, or I will shoot! Do it now!"

The figure froze in place briefly before the revolver was released and dropped onto the ground. Wilbert rushed towards the assailant and forced them to the ground, then retrieved the weapon and inserted it under his belt. "Put your hands behind your back!" Wilbert commanded as he pushed his knee down firmly to hold the assailant in place. As he was about to place his handcuffs on the assailant's wrists, Wilbert heard a familiar voice pleading, "You're hurting me, dear."

It was his wife, Rachael.

Intense emotion overtook Wilbert as he tried in every way to tell himself it could not possibly be her. He released his grip and helped her to her feet. "You...!Rachael...it cannot be you..." was all he could bring himself to utter. "Not you..for the love of God...not you!"

Rachael knew that her murdering spree had now officially ended. "Let's go home now and I'll explain everything to you once we get situated," she told him. "Then you can decide what's to be done with me." She refused to answer any of his questions along the way.

Inside the barn, the life-long member of the Shaker religious sect continued working, totally oblivious to everything that had transpired outside. The man known only as Brother Jacobs would now live to see another sunrise.

The young woman who Brother Jacobs came upon in the Edward's kitchen was in fact his own brother's illegitimate daughter, Sandra Lawrence.

CHAPTER 20

Her Confession

Deputy Marshal Wilbert Vance was in a complete daze when he and Rachael finally arrived home. After hanging up their coats, Rachael went into their child's bedroom to check on little Mary Louise. "She's sound asleep," Rachael said.

"You went off and left her unprotected. What if there had been a fire or something," Wilbert said in an angry voice. She could offer no excuse and seated herself alone on their sofa. He sat down in his stuffed chair across from her. The two stared at each other for a few seconds until she began to speak.

"When you married me, I told you my name was Rachael Marley from Fort Wayne, but my real name is Julie Collins. I am the sister of the innocent boy those awful men lynched in that tree and also murdered my grandfather, Roscoe Sawyer. It was my grandmother, Vivian Sawyer, who went mad and placed the curse on those men and the land. The woman you know as Mother Marley is actually my aunt, Wilma Sawyer."

Wilbert's eyes became enlarged upon hearing all this and he felt his mind spinning out of control. His entire world was crumbling right before his tearful eyes.

"Before that awful night in 1885, I was simply a happy young girl, excited at the prospects of my family moving to Alexandra, where my Aunt Wilma would help care for Grandmother. My grandfather was a kind, hard-working man who loved Grandmother deeply, but due to her losing her mental faculties, knew we needed help. At that time, she only had moments where she acted strangely. We had arrived just outside of what was then Harrisburg and camped out. Grandmother, my brother Stanley, and I soon began to explore the town. You see, my older brother had mental issues stemming from his birth and though he was a teenager, Stanley was probably only five years old inside his mind. He liked to play games and imagined himself a cowboy or a wild Indian.

"I had met a new friend here by the name of Cynthia Rains. Her father was the grocer where we shopped that day. Unfortunately, my brother acted up and attempted to grab her. Later that evening, he followed me back and in front of her parents said something about taking her as his own.

"Late that night, a group of four men entered our camp and grabbed my brother, claiming he had raped and strangled Cynthia. One of the men was her father. We knew Stanley was incapable of such a hideous thing and that he had returned to camp even before me. My grandfather pleaded with them that they had made a terrible mistake, but they beat him until his heart gave out and died. Grandmother and I pleaded but to no avail. They hung my poor brother from a nearby dead tree. Grandmother's mind snapped and that is when she placed a curse on them and the land. Now I was all alone as my grandmother was incapable of helping me get us to Alexandria. I somehow managed to eventually find my way to my aunt's home and I told her of the terrible events in Harrisburg. She took us in, but grandmother's mind became even worse, with only periods of lucidness. It was during those periods that she told us of our responsibility to avenge the murder of family members. We each swore to do just that, no matter how long it took to accomplish justice. In time grandmother passed away, and Aunt Wilma and I worried that one day we might become just like her.

"Another year came and went. Aunt Wilma decided she was tired of running a boarding house and sold out. With no place in particular to go, we decided Fort Wayne might hold our best opportunities. We boarded a train northward, which stopped at, of all places, Jonesboro Station, here in Harrisburg. All of those ugly memories I had tried so hard to forget came flooding back to me. By the time our train returned to its journey, I made a silent vow to myself that as soon as I came of age, I would return and seek out the killers of my family and destroy them. I also decided to change my name to Rachael, a name I had often heard and loved, that way I could never be associated with my real name of Julie. After we settled in, Aunt Wilma met a policeman and the two fell in love. He became very important in our lives and I grew to love him dearly; allowing me to call him Father. In time I began to use his last name of Marley as my own. I was now Rachael Marley of Fort Wayne.

"Unfortunately, he died in the line of duty, and death took hold of my subconscious. At that point I was an adult and ready to find a way to bring those killers to justice. I boarded a train to what was now being called Gas City. Do you remember, darling, that is when I first met and fell in love with you, dear husband? Still, the thoughts of revenge never seemed to leave my mind. After speaking with several people, I learned that the grocer Thaddeus Rains had taken his family to live in Kokomo and he had been killed in an accident. The woman I had spoken to knew all the facts that I needed. It seemed his brother had died soon after as well as the neighbor. So, three of the four men had met their fate, no doubt as payback for what they did to Grandfather and Stanley. Unfortunately, nobody knew the name of the stranger who took part in the lynching. By then, we were married and I was happier than I'd ever been. And then it happened; I saw the face of the stranger here in town. Older yes, a bit heavier and grayer, yes, but now wearing a beard, but it was a face whose features had burned deep into my very soul. His name was Roland Edwards Sr. I immediately wrote to Aunt Wilma and informed her.

"I had heard all the stories going around about my grandmother's curse and the bad luck and death associated with that land. I, of course, had nothing to do with any of it but it helped keep the stories alive. Now Edwards had reappeared into my life and only his painful death would satisfy my lust for revenge. I learned he had purchased two lots; his, and the one next to it where the hanging tree once stood. I determined that some Indian chanting at night might start the process, as there had been stories of people hearing it. Since you were working the night shift, I found it easy to do. Then, I went to a sale and purchased a small child's drum and used it along with my chanting. From the stories I heard, it was working, but I needed to accomplish more, much more. One night I entered his barn and using a wrench I located on his workbench, loosened a wheel nut on his carriage. I was overjoyed to learn of his bad accident and especially of his broken hip! Now the final murderer of my family had to spend his days sitting in a wheelchair, but I wanted to cause him more pain and suffering.

"After watching Edward's wife's schedule, I learned she went to church alone on Sundays and left the rear door of their home unlocked. I entered the home with a lead water pipe I had found in the neighbor's trash. I crept silently from their kitchen and saw the back of him looking out a living room window. Now I had the dirty murderer in my grasp! I twirled his wheelchair around and held the pipe ready to strike. "It was YOU who put the noose around my brother's neck for a crime he didn't commit! Now it is YOUR time to pay for your crime!" I yelled. Fear appeared in his evil face as he began to whimper and pleaded for his life and finally admitted that HE was the real rapist of Cynthia. I demanded to hear more.

'I don't know why I did such a terrible thing to that girl,' he cried. 'But it has haunted my dreams ever since, along with the hanging of your brother to cover up for my crime. I waited a fair amount of time before I returned here, only to discover my three accomplices were no longer alive to recognize me. After that, I became a wealthy man. Miss, I can give you money,' he pleaded. 'Lots of money!'

"Wilbert, I was so enraged with his attempt to buy me off, that I spun him around and struck him as hard as I could on the head with the pipe. He slumped down in his chair and

I suspected I had killed him and I was so happy. In the small hallway was a door that opened to the cellar. I opened it and pushed his wheelchair to its entrance. "This will help you on your way to Hell!" I shouted as I pushed him down the stairs. His chair crashed on the bottom floor. After feeling his pulse, I saw that he was dead. Wilbert, I had such a sense of relief and could almost hear my grandmother congratulating me. I then left the same way I came and returned home. But my dreams were not peaceful. I could hear my grandmother telling me that much more needed to happen, and the land now occupied must be purged in blood. I realized then that I was not finished." Rachael got up to get a glass of water. "May I bring you one, sweetheart?" Wilbert didn't reply and soon she returned to the sofa to continue her story.

"Now it was time to continue my night chanting and drums whenever I could get away at night. Just by chance, I was walking by one day when I overhear a group of boys teasing one about being afraid and daring him to remain on the empty lot that night. I felt that Providence had provided an opportunity for me to continue the fear generated by the curse. After Edwards had gone and met the Devil, I placed some objects inside his unlocked gardening shed. One of those was a nice-looking Indian tomahawk I had made after seeing how in a magazine. The boy was just another way of spreading fear. After killing him I decided to leave it behind."

Wilbert appeared sick to his stomach after hearing all of this. "I just cannot believe you are capable of cold-blooded murder," he told her.

"Not murder, Darling. Revenge! I had to continue as long as Grandmother wanted me to. Can't you understand that?" She took another sip of water.

"So, to continue, I decided to pay a visit to Mother Edwards and attempt to scare the bejeesus out of her. That night I told you I was going to visit a sick friend, but instead, I went to her property and grabbed my ghost outfit. She was over visiting her son and daughter-in-law, so I snuck in the back door and went upstairs to await her return. It only took a few seconds to get the eye holes lined up for my eyes and when I heard her enter, I donned the costume and waited. I heard her coming up the stairs, and when I heard the floor creak, I jumped out at her. She screamed and fell backward partway down the stairs. I was then concerned I may be trapped upstairs, but when she seemed to have passed out, I escaped.

"Getting back to Edward Jr. and his wife, I hounded them with chanting and sometimes wore the sheet with a lit candle underneath carefully placed away from the fabric. It gave the appearance of glowing. I even scared myself!"

"So why did you use my twenty-two pistol to shoot at Brother Jacobs?"

"I think you know why. I got careless and should have removed my equipment out of the gardening shed. When he got close, I hoped he would be scared away and leave for good. But he didn't. Last night, Grandmother came to me in a dream and told me I was to shoot that old man in his workshop when nobody was around. When you started your stakeout, I naturally assumed it was over at the Edwards property, not over in North Jonesboro. You sure fooled me, sweetheart. So now, the decision to lock me up or not rests entirely on you, my husband. In my next dream, I will inform Grandmother that our work here is finished. I will then return to the sweet wife and good mother that you knew. Our work is finished. Do what you will with me, Deputy Vance."

"So, what do I call you then? Julie?"

She smiled. "Darling, my name is Rachael Vance, your loving wife and the mother of our beautiful little daughter. I am going to bed now. Come if you like, or do what your job requires. Goodnight."

Wilbert sat up all night lost in thought, and the next night, and the next...

CHAPTER 21

Present Day Gas City Museum

Paul Middleton finally completed reading the last page of the copied document and set it to the side as he awaited a response from the two historical society members. "Oh, my God," was all that Cecil Beck managed to say.

"That is a fascinating slice of history. Hearing it made me feel as if I was witnessing the past for myself," Wanda Westland replied. "I wish your ancestor had told us what happened next. That information isn't anywhere in our records here at the museum."

Paul smiled. "I can tell you as it's part of our family folklore. Wilbert Vance never told a living soul or turned his wife in for her part in the killings. They stayed together as husband and wife and in 1903, adopted a newborn son whom they named Justin, after his best friend, and a two-year-old daughter they renamed Virginia. Unfortunately, young Justin was killed in WW-1. From what I remember my grandmother saying, Rachael never got over the loss and her mind began to slowly deteriorate and Wilbert cared for her until the very end. She died sometime in the later 1920s, but I don't remember exactly when."

"What a terrible secret for a lawman to have kept to himself all those years. Now I understand why he documented everything in the ledger. It was probably his way of making final amends," Cecil replied.

"Back then, people called it 'hardening of the arteries' and didn't understand what happened to the elderly. I can see now why some thought that Vivian was a witch or just plain crazy. Today we know that terrible medical condition as Dementia," Wanda stated.

"I have one last piece of family history, but there's no way of proving it. My grandma said that Justin Blake retired as the Gas City marshal in 1911 after contracting tuberculosis. I was told that during his going-away party, Justin said that his deepest regret was not solving this case. I was told that Wilbert then broke down in tears. If so, nobody could suspect the real reason. As you probably know, he assumed the position of marshal and kept it until his death in 1933."

"I'm sure Rachael was present at that event. I would have liked to have seen her face when it was brought up," Cecil said. "You know, it's funny. I just recalled a story from my youth that my classmates spoke about hearing wild Indians on nights of a full moon. I haven't thought about that story in many years. Those old ghost stories were handed down generation to generation."

"Or," Wanda said with a smile, "Stanley is still out there, somewhere, playing wild Indian." That statement brought a light chuckle out of everyone.

"Well, I guess I need to be moseying back home now. I've taken up too much of your time already. Here is the ledger and its copy if you want it. If not, I'll take it back with me," Paul said. They most certainly wanted it.

"Mr. Middleton," Wanda said, "I want to personally thank you for donating this valuable piece of Gas City history to our museum. At this point, I don't know what the society board will want to do with it, but I can assure you it will create great interest among our members."

Paul left the building and started driving home, wondering if he had done the right thing or not. *Our history, whether pleasant or not, should not be erased, amended, or kept hidden away,* he told himself. *I'll let those who come after us make the final decision. I think that's the way Wilbert Vance would have wanted it anyway.*

HISTORICAL TIDBITS OF LOCAL INTEREST ON GAS CITY, INDIANA

The following headlines appeared in the November 4, 1901 edition of the Marion Leader newspaper:

The Gas City Bridge Goes Up in Smoke

The Jonesboro-Gas City bridge was completely destroyed by fire this afternoon. The bridge caught fire shortly after 1:30 p.m. and in less than an hour, it was a mass of ruins. The fire first started in the dwelling house of Herbert Daily, which stood south of the bridge. While an attempt was made to extinguish the flames here, the fire had gained such headway that the bucket brigade, which had been formed, was entirely powerless. A stiff northerly wind carried the sparks over to the covered bridge, the roof took fire in several places at one time, and within a few moments, the old landmark was wiped out of existence.

Some of those who had started to fight the fire at the dwelling now left and made efforts to save the bridge, but their work was to no avail; the wooden structure burned like tinder. The men who were fighting the fire drew back away from the hot, scorching flames and sought safety with the crowd that had gathered on the riverbank. It was a grand spectacle as the timbers gave way, and the rails of the trolley fell into the water with parts of the burning structure. In about an hour after the fire started in the dwelling, nothing but charred ends of the structure close to the foundation of the bridge were left to mark the spot. The bridge burned close to the water's edge.

Two short stories to Introduce

A NEW MAIN CHARACTER:

Captain Benjamin Stewart, Grant County
Deputy Sheriff Crime Scene Investigator

THE STRANGE CASE OF BETH ANN WAVERLY

The Cast of Main Characters

Benjamin Stewart	Crime Scene Investigator
Hugo Barns	Investigator's Assistant
Joseph Epstein	Husband
Ruth Epstein	Wife
Beth Ann Waverly	Fire Victim
Hershel Dent	Beth Ann's Brother
"Pickpocket" Pete Hampton	Thug Friend of Hershel
Joshua Sterling	Tobacconist
Sergeant Clark	Marion Policeman
Philip DuPont	Assistant Fire Chief
Doctor Walter Shelby	Grant County Medical Examiner
Jacks Are Wild Saloon	A Drinking Establishment

Chapter 1

May 2, 1905
Marion, Indiana

It was the start of another busy work week for detective Captain Benjamin Stewart, who had worked his way up through the ranks the hard way. Four years ago, as a member of the Marion Metropolitan Police, he found himself at the scene of a murder and casually pointed out two important clues that the old detective assigned to the case had overlooked. Though nothing was said at that moment, Stewart's keen eyes and power of observation didn't go unnoticed when reported later to his superiors. When the old detective soon retired, Benjamin Stewart was offered the vacant position of a deputy sheriff in the Grant County Sheriff's Department with the title; crime scene investigator. A bachelor at age 31, he stood at six foot one and weighed in at one hundred eighty-five pounds. Noted for his large handlebar mustache and neat appearance, he was considered very handsome by the ladies who sought to catch his eye. His place of residence was at the luxurious downtown Spencer Hotel. Constructed in 1856, it had recently undergone a major renovation. The hotel offered clean rooms, bathrooms, elegant dining, livery service, and office space on the first floor. The hotel was more than accommodating in providing a permanent residence for him inside room # 311.

People were often confused over the difference between a policeman and a deputy sheriff. A policeman is solely responsible for the city or town in which he works, while a deputy sheriff works within all areas of the county and works side-by-side with the police, if needed, during criminal investigations. While some Hoosier cities have a bitter rivalry between both branches of law enforcement, none existed in Grant County. The willing assistance provided by the Marion Metropolitan Police had greatly added to the successful prosecution of many local criminals. Also, crime scene investigators dressed in a suit and not a uniform.

Captain Stewart had just finished his morning breakfast in the hotel's elegant dining room when a familiar face approached his table. "What's gotten you out so early this morning, Hugo?" The new arrival was Hugo Barns, an investigator assistant who worked with Stewart on most criminal investigations. His job was to support the investigator with fieldwork, collecting police evidence and fingerprints, interviewing witnesses, filing reports, and anything else required.

"Good morning, sir," he said. "I'm sorry to bother you at the breakfast table." Stewart motioned for the man to have a seat. Despite his best efforts, Stewart was unable to persuade Hugo to be a little less formal when not in mixed company.

"I've finished. What do you have?"

"An accidental killing it appears, sir. Happened sometime early this morning."

Hugo Barns, Investigator's Assistant

Hugo Barns was quite a character. A small and unassuming man, Stewart's investigator assistant was one year younger than himself and possessed a dapper appearance. He possessed a way of appearing less intimidating to a suspect, while at the same time, the ability to read a suspect or victim's body language. More than once, Hugo had successfully steered Stewart's attention toward or away from an individual. Hugo was single and lived in a boarding house in the upper section of town.

The last few weeks had been quite busy with a series of home break-ins occurring in town. With milder temperatures arriving, homeowners were anxious to leave their bedroom windows cracked open a bit at night. That was all a bandit required to silently enter a window and go through the pants pockets of men and the handbags of their wives in search of valuables. Word of the robberies spread quickly through each neighborhood, and as a result, more than a few homeowners now slept with a loaded weapon near them, ready to use at a moment's notice. Unfortunately, this public fear seemed to have led to the early morning shooting incident.

Hugo continued. "From what I just learned, the police received a report of an early-morning residential shooting at the home of Joseph Epstein, age 41, in the two hundred block of Nebraska Street. Arriving officers discovered his body lying within their bedroom and a fired Colt 45 revolver lying on the floor next to the bed. His wife stated her husband had left early in the evening to enjoy a couple of drinks with his friends. Later she had gone to bed alone, awoke with a start, heard a figure bump into a piece of bedroom furniture, and thinking it to be a burglar, shot several times. The police have only been there a short time. It seems there was a delay in reporting the incident."

Now ready to begin their day, Captain Stewart grabbed his hat as both proceeded to exit the hotel and walked to the nearby stable where Benjamin Stewart housed his automobile. It was a bright red 1904 Studebaker Model C, made in

South Bend, Indiana. He had ordered the optional cloth roof to protect him from heavy rain. He had used it very sparingly during the winter months due to its light grip in snowy conditions. On those days, the department's horses served the purpose. Hugo turned the crank located on the front of the car, as Benjamin applied the spark throttle. After only two cranks, the automobile fired up. Hugo entered the passenger seat and the men pulled out of the building and headed the car towards Nebraska Street.

The brick streets were beginning to fill up with morning activity as the small automobile made its way. By now, most horses seemed to have become somewhat accustomed to the noisy contraptions puttering about, but Captain Steward tried to avoid coming too close and startling the poor animals. The sky was clear with only a few morning clouds, promising the start of another fine day of weather. Born into a family of some wealth, Steward displayed no hesitation in using his vehicle in the performance of his job.

"That's it there," Hugo said, as the vehicle came to a halt on the dirt street. With two horse-drawn police paddy wagons already parked outside, Hugo's statement proved unnecessary. Entering, there was an array of activities as the photographer was doing his best in asking the policemen to step out of the crime scene. The city of Marion didn't pay a full-time photographer on its payroll, instead entering into an on-call contract arrangement with a local studio.

"Make way, gentlemen," the photographer could be heard saying as he tried to photograph the body from all angles.

A police sergeant that Stewart knew only by his last name of Clark saw them arriving and stepped out into the hallway to speak privately. "Morning Captain. Her name is Ruth Epstein, age 37. She freely admits to shooting her husband but claims she thought he was a prowler. We found a Colt 45 on the floor where she dropped it by the bed. All six rounds had been fired." That made Stewart's eyebrows raise with surprise.

"Thanks, Clark. We'll need to interview her later. Where is she?"

"She is sitting in the kitchen drinking coffee."

"Has the medical examiner arrived yet?"

"Yes sir, just before you did. He's in there now with the body," Clark said as he left to return to his work.

Captain Stewart and Hugo Barns entered the bedroom. The body of a man lying face down in a pool of dark blood was being attended to by Doctor Shelby, a trained pathologist. Steward stooped to where the doctor was kneeling and asked, "How does it look, Doc?"

"Multiple gunshot wounds, two shots to the chest and abdomen as well as those in the back. I can have you a medical report right after lunch." That satisfied Captain Stewart who then examined the room from all angles, the open window, the marked location where the weapon was found, and paced the distance from the bed to where the body had laid. Finally, he was ready to speak with Mrs. Epstein.

Both officers instinctively sized up the female shooter. She was sitting at a small table clothed in a bathrobe. "Mrs. Epstein, I am Captain Stewart and this is Officer Barns. We're from the Grant County sheriff's department." He waited to receive some form of acknowledgment but received no reply. "I need you to start at the beginning and tell us what happened here last night, ma'am."

Some visible anger flashed over her face. "I've already told the police what happened. Go ask them, I'm tired of talking about it."

Captain Stewart maintained his poker face as he replied, "I need to hear it from you, ma'am. Start at the beginning."

Seeing that these two new men in suits didn't back down, she began. "Well, alright if you insist. Last night Joe, ah, that's my husband, said he was going out for a few drinks with the boys and wouldn't be gone long. I waited and waited until it was late, but he still hadn't returned. So, when I started getting sleepy, I put on my gown, opened the curtains a bit, then raised the window for some cooler air. You see I sleep better when it's cooler and…"

"Yes ma'am, please continue."

"I don't have any idea how long I was asleep when I heard a chair being knocked over in our bedroom. I awoke with a start and through the darkness, I could just make out the figure of an intruder moving about. We had heard the stories about burglars, so Joe got out his revolver and showed me how to use it. I don't remember anything after the first shot. I was so terrified by what just occurred, that I crawled under the covers to await my husband's return. But as soon as the dawn light arrived, I could make out the appearance of the intruder and saw it to be my husband. I tried to shake him but he didn't move. That's when I called the police. I guess that's all I can tell you."

Stewart wasn't quite satisfied. "So, you are saying you shot from your bed and didn't leave it until dawn? Is that what you are telling us?" Mrs. Epstein said that was so.

"How many shots did you fire?"

"A couple, I think. I just don't remember for sure. I dropped the revolver onto the floor by our bed, so you can check it if you like."

This time Hugo asked, "How long have you been married?"

"In July it will be... ah, would have been one year. How soon until I can arrange for his burial? I have nothing left here in Marion and wish to return to my mother in Kokomo."

"We'll let you know," Mrs. Epstein, Stewart said. Both men then stepped outside to speak.

"She's not telling us everything she knows, Captain," Hugo said.

"I agree. In her story she mentioned a chair being knocked over. The only chair I saw in the bedroom sat in the corner of the room. It appeared to have a dress laid across the back, so I'm guessing it was the dress she wore yesterday since she was still wearing a bathrobe and slippers. We might as well return to the office to finish up our paperwork while we await the medical examiner's report. I need time to think anyway."

The Grant County Jail in Marion

Advertised as the most modern jail in the state of Indiana, The Grant County Jail was equipped with sixty cells to house prisoners. In the image above, the structure on the left was the eleven-room family living residence for the elected county sheriff. The rear jail contained three floors and hosted four guard towers. Its first floor housed male prisoners. The second floor was for juveniles, while the third housed female prisoners, as well as a hospital ward. The facility also possessed three specially equipped cells for unruly prisoners. The basement contained a washroom, storeroom, fuel room, kitchen, and heating plant. This structure could be entered through either east or west entrances.

Built between the two structures, but not visible above, was a two-story administrative facility housing the guards, interrogation rooms, armory, and offices for the Grant County deputy sheriffs, as well as other lawmen. Captain Stewart entered his office, located on the second floor, and began working on the endless stack of paperwork required for his job, and waited for the medical report to be delivered.

* * * * * * * * *

Later that afternoon, it arrived and Captain Stewart read through it carefully. "Well," an anxious Hugo asked. "What does it say?"

"Here, let me show you," the detective said as he walked over to a small chalkboard on the wall often used in case studies. Picking up a piece of chalk, he drew a rough sketch of the crime scene. He then placed a small X in the bed where Mrs. Epstein had sat up and fired from. "Alright, Hugo. Here is the body of the deceased lying on its stomach near the center of the bedroom floor. Earlier I paced out the distance from her position in bed to the body at just under ten feet. The medical examiner states that after examining the paths of the two bullets fired into the chest and abdomen area, he determined that both had entered horizontally."

Stewart then drew two lines in chalk vertically upward through the body towards the ceiling. "Are you with me?" Hugo nodded he understood. "So here is a body that fell flat on its stomach. The report states that four more slugs were found in various locations inside the back that traveled at a near forty-five-degree angle downward." Stewart then drew four lines at that angle to represent the four shots. "As you can see, it would have been impossible for four bullets to travel from her gun at this angle had Mrs. Epstein remained in bed as she claimed. No, after the first two shots, she had to get up to stand next to her husband's body, shooting downward to achieve that angle. Her story is false and we now have probable cause that she deliberately shot her husband."

Soon, the evidence was presented to a county judge who approved an arrest warrant. Mrs. Epstein was taken into custody and placed within the segregated third floor of the jail.

The following day, Ruth Epstein was brought before the court and charged with the first-degree murder of her husband, Joseph Epstein, and provided with legal counsel. She immediately broke down in tears. Later, after conferring with her counsel, an offer was made for a complete confession and the implication of her accomplice, Philip Silo of Marion, age 38, in exchange for a lesser second-degree indictment. The offer was accepted by the county prosecutor and an arrest warrant was issued for Silo. Within days, he was discovered in hiding and charged with aiding and abetting in the murder of Joseph Epstein. It was later learned that Ruth Epstein, after realizing her mistake in marrying her husband, turned to an old boyfriend for help. When word of the home break-ins began to circulate, Philip Silo suggested she use that ploy to rid herself of her husband, and that nobody would ever suspect her. Ruth Epstein had allowed her lust for another man and her frustrations to impede her judgment by leaping from her bed and emptying the remaining cartridges almost point-blank into his back. Had she only fired the first two rounds, and improved her story a bit, perhaps she might have gotten away with it.

Someone once said that crime doesn't pay, and that was certainly the case for Ruth Epstein, who was eventually sentenced to twenty-five years to life. Her boyfriend Philip Silo was sentenced to ten years for assisting in the murder.

Chapter 2

Beth Ann Waverly

Widow Mrs. Beth Ann Waverly    Her brother, Hershel Dent

Life had not always been unhappy for Beth Ann Waverly. Born and raised locally, she had met and married a young man whom people said was going places in life. Thomas Waverly had a successful knack for making and investing his money. When the couple first met, he was a clerk working in a hardware store. Within five years he and his wife, the former Beth Ann Dent, owned the hardware store. From that point forward, the couple saved every penny they could and purchased a small house for rental investment income. The couple had no children. By the time Thomas succumbed to a heart attack three years ago, they had acquired a total of nine rental properties. Now financially secure for life, but feeling alone and abandoned, Beth Ann's younger brother Hershel Dent entered the picture. He was more than willing to move into her home and assist his lonely sister by spending her money.

Considered to be nearly worthless by many locals, Hershel Dent had been in and out of jail all his life. Upon hearing of Thomas's death and sensing the perfect opportunity, he showed up unexpectedly on his sister's doorstep and never left. Anxious for the company, she welcomed her brother in. Not one to work for his living when stealing proved easier, Dent soon began pilfering his sister's jewelry to fulfill his need for whiskey. Eventually, little by little, most of her expensive items around the house disappeared; this only contributed to the deep depression Beth Ann was experiencing. Soon, she joined her brother in drink, starting in the early afternoon, and continuing onward until collapsing into bed. She stopped going outside and ordered her groceries and cases of whiskey to be delivered. Never one to be considered thin in stature, her increased drinking habit led to a huge gain in weight. Her depression only mounted as she found no comfort in her brother's presence but was unable to convince him to leave. She knew full well that he was using her and was reminded of the old saying: feed a stray cat...own a stray cat. Her only escape in life now was found inside the bottle.

* * * * * * * * *

"Pickpocket Pete" Hampton

"Are you serious?" Fellow thug and drinking partner Pete Hampton replied in astonishment to Hershel Dent. "She's your sister, for crying out loud!" It was not every day that someone asked you to come up with a fool-proof plan to murder their sister.

"I ain't foolin' none, Pete. When it comes ta money, nothin' else matters. It ain't like we was close. She got lots of cash in some stupid bank and rental houses, but when I asked her fer half of it, she told me ta go jump off a bridge! You bein' smart and all can come up with a plan to get rid of her so I can inherit everythin' she has. Then, I'll give you a third of her money and properties. You'll be rich! Folks here know my record with da cops and I need one of dem there alibies since nobody would suspect you of anything, as you ain't got no motive."

The criminal locals knew as "Pickpocket Pete" said he would give the proposition serious thought and get back with his friend shortly. A simple murder or fatal fire might easily cause the cops to suspect foul play and eventually lead back to him. That wouldn't do at all. *The old lady never leaves her house, so I cannot arrange for an accident to befall her elsewhere,* he told himself. *No, something original had to be planned, something completely different that would confuse the local authorities while clearing the way for Hershel's inheritance.*

"I'm not committing myself to anything, you understand, but I would like to gain entry inside her home and scope out the layout for myself," he replied.

"Dat's easy. She drinks herself ta sleep most nights ah sitting in her rocker or at da table."

Pickpocket Pete smiled. "Tonight, you need to encourage her to drink heavily, but don't let her pass out downstairs. Make her go to her bedroom. Once the coast is clear, flicker the lights in the dining room window to signal me the coast is clear."

Hershel made a sour face. "She's so fat it's hard ta get her butt up dem stairs!"

"If you want my help, you'll have to do your part. I'll be watching once it gets dark for your signal." Pickpocket Pete was a noted reader and felt that the answer to their problem may very well lay within the pages of one of his many books. He returned home and began his search. After a couple of hours, he was about to give up when his eyes fell upon an older book he had been given and never bother to open. Its title was: The Anatomy of Drunkenness, by Robert Machish. It soon caught his interest as he read all thirty short examples within its medical texts. About halfway through, he remembered another example and removed a book from the shelf. It was written by one of his favorite authors, Charles Dickens. That book was entitled: Bleak House. Its storyline quickly came back to him. *I now have the answer*, he told himself. Pickpocket Pete Hampton sat back anxiously and awaited the appointed hour.

* * * * * * * * *

Darkness had fallen as he waited outside. Soon, a bright light flickered behind a first-floor window. It was their signal. Pickpocket Pete was met at the front door and quickly entered. "Are you absolutely positive you want to go through with all this?" he asked. "Once we start, there's no turning back." Hershel Dent nodded he was all-in.

"She's upstairs passed out across her bed. What do we do now?"

Pickpocket Pete walked past him and began to intently study every downstairs room. He then returned to the dining room, pulled out a chair from the table, and climbed up to examine the large curtains hanging over two windows. Hershel was very confused why his friend cared anything at all about curtains. Now satisfied, Pickpocket Pete replaced the chair and examined the electric light hanging over the round drum table, then proceeded towards the picture hanging on the wall. He then asked Hershel if there was a measuring yardstick in the home. It took a bit of looking, but one was found. With it, Pickpocket Pete took the full measurements of both window interiors and wrote the information into a small notebook. "Do you know if there's a stepladder out in your barn?"

Hershel said there was. "What's so important about curtains, pictures, and ladders anyway? I thought you was ah gonna help me get rid of dat old cow!"

Pickpocket Pete smiled. "I am, and in fact, it's going to happen this Saturday night. Today is Tuesday so it will give me adequate time to get things ready. But you need to know, what I'm planning might very well burn this house to the ground."

Hershel said it was probably insured anyway and he didn't care one way or the other. Pickpocket Pete then explained exactly what was about to happen. The expression on Hershel's face indicated he was confused, but it didn't matter anyway. "The main thing is that once we set the fire, we need to head straight to a noisy saloon, drink, and pick a fight with a few other men so we'll be arrested," he said. "That way, we have the perfect alibi."

Hershel smiled. "Yea, I get it. With us bein' locked up in jail overnight, we can't be charged with killin' her. But, tell me again, what this thing's being called?"

Pickpocket Pete replied. "It's called Spontaneous Human Combustion."

CHAPTER 3

The Plan Comes Together

Pickpocket Pete Hampton felt he had everything figured out to the letter. If his plan failed, and too much oxygen entered the room, the house would simply burn to the ground. Either way, the problem would be solved and the promised financial windfall would be his. Trying to make all of this work out successfully was now a greater challenge than simple arson. *These local yokels won't have a clue as to the real reason for the fire and my successful effort will make the history book for sure!*

Pete drove his wagon over to the nearby lumberyard and purchased two sheets of three-quarter-inch plywood. Then, inside his workshop, Pete cut both sheets to the size specifications he had measured of the two windows inside the dining room of the old lady's house. Then after lunch, he rode out of town to a local pig farmer he knew and brought back three five-gallon cans of animal fat tissue. Once home, he used the blunt end of a two-by-four and began the process of mashing up the pieces of fat into a white soft paste goo. This took several days to complete and Pete had to cover the cans to lower the terrible smell and keep the flies away. By Thursday, all was ready.

Then on Friday evening, once the old lady had passed out, Pete met up with Hershel in the alley behind the home's rear barn. Both sheets of plywood were brought inside it, as well as the containers of stinky fat.

"What is that God awful smell?" Hershel demanded to know.

"Don't worry about it. I just wanted to get everything in place here for tomorrow night," Pete replied. Along with these items, he also brought along another pair of pants and a shirt inside a small bag, as well as a screwdriver. "Now make sure she has plenty of whiskey in the house. I need her to pass out downstairs in that dining room. As for killing her…I'll leave that up to you to perform, but make sure you don't leave any blood on or below the table. Afterward, place her on her back up next to the wall." Hershel showed no emotion and nodded; he would see to it. "Have a small table lamp on to allow me just enough light to work in. Have the plywood, the step ladder, and all the containers of pig fat inside before you signal me. Use care not to spill any of it. Leave my bag of clothing in the barn as I'll change out there afterward. Oh ya, I'll need a stack of clean towels too. Just put them on that round drum table."

The Curse of the Hanging Tree

Hershel agreed and everything was now set. "Let's hope for another foggy night tomorrow," Pete said.

* * * * * * * * *

The powers of evil granted their wish, as a light fog began forming shortly after dark. This would be very helpful in hiding any smoke, but of no use at all if open flames broke out. Pete had parked his wagon a block away and approached the house. Seeing the signal light in the window, he entered and was told everything was ready. Hershel then left the murder scene and proceeded on foot to his favorite drinking establishment, Jacks Are Wild Saloon, located near the railroad depot. It was a wild and wooly saloon, full of hard-drinking men, and would serve their purposes nicely as it was often patrolled by the police.

Pete took a few seconds to examine his friend's handiwork. There, just as instructed, the body of Beth Ann Waverly lay next to the wall facing upward. The large bloodspot near her heart indicated she had most likely been stabbed. Now Pete began to prepare his work. Using the step ladder, he positioned it under each tall window and removed each set of curtains and rods. These were placed inside the living room. He then removed wall pictures, the doily on the center of the round drum table, and relocated the small table holding a candlestick telephone and other items to the same location. Since the telephone cord was not long, the telephone was placed as far away as it would reach. Pete then lifted each piece of measured plywood, while inserting them into both window frames making sure they fit snugly. They did. The plywood was there to prevent the expected flames from fracturing the glass, thus allowing a new supply of oxygen into the room. If this happened, the fire would quickly spread from the room and engulf the entire house. Luckily for their plan, the dining room contained two doors, one leading into the kitchen and the other into the living room. There, in the kitchen, he noticed a bloody ice pick lying in the sink. Disgusted at his friend's clumsiness, Pete washed off the blood and returned it to the utility drawer. *I'm sure happy I caught that.* He then grabbed a few towels off the table, shut the door into the living room, and began stuffing the towels underneath it. Satisfied that no new air could enter from that direction, Pete took the remaining towels and placed them in the kitchen. He would do the same to that door once he was leaving. Now it was time for the real fun to begin.

With careful deliberation, Pete began to pour each container of pig fat goo all over the torso and head of the deceased. Its natural thickness allowed for a heavy buildup and quickly saturated the upper parts of the torso. The legs were left free of fat deliberately on purpose. Once each container was emptied, they were placed outside the kitchen door on the grass. These would be retrieved when he made his escape. Giving everything a final look over, an old newspaper was wadded up, placed on the liquified fatty materials, and lit. Pete remained until he saw that the combustible fat had ignited. Many might have thought to use kerosene or lamp oil instead, but their residue could be detected later by a police chemical analysis. Pete was surprised at the intensity of the flames and quickly left, shut the door, and stuffed the remaining towels underneath. He exited the house, grabbed up the empty containers, and placed them inside his wagon. They would be disposed of somewhere while he was on his way home. Pete then returned to the barn to hide and watch. *Hopefully*, he thought, *for my plan to work, the intense fire will extinguish itself after the supply of oxygen in the room is used up. If not...*

The minutes passed by slowly as the smell of smoke penetrated the air. After fifteen minutes, the house remained standing and with no sign of flames visible. *Either it's working or the fire burned itself out.* The urge to investigate was strong, but Pete knew not to enter prematurely and in so doing, introduce new oxygen into the room. Heavier smoke was becoming more prominent, and he hoped it wouldn't become noticeable by any of the neighbors who were thankfully inside for the night. The hours passed by.

* * * * * * * * *

Pete lit a match and looked at his pocket watch. It showed the time to be ten-fifteen. *Enough time had passed.* Pete returned inside the house, where he was met by a thick wall of terrible-smelling smoke. Now was the start of another dangerous part of his plan. If the smoke was noticed by a neighbor who came to investigate, he would say that he too arrived for that purpose. Luckily, the heavy smoke went unnoticed in the foggy night air. Pete entered the kitchen and approached the closed dining-room door. Feeling it, he realized it was warm to the touch. He removed the bottom towels and opened the door. Thick clouds of heavy smoke filled the air and he couldn't see anything. The horrible smell made him gag. *I need to let this place air out*, he thought as he returned to the barn.

Once the escaping smoke had thinned, Pete placed the screwdriver in his pocket and grabbed the ladder. *I wish I had thought to bring leather gloves.* As he carried his equipment into the dining room, he lit a match to the small candle he had placed inside his pocket. Lighting it, his eyes adjusted to its flame as he looked towards the body. He was horrified by what he saw; a pair of legs from the knees were mostly all that remained. His stomach began churning and dry heaves started in his stomach from the horrible odor of burnt flesh. It was nearly overpowering. *I'm glad I didn't eat tonight or I would be puking my guts out right now.* Pete took a few seconds to examine the area below the windows. The flames had indeed scorched the walls, chairs, and ceiling. The two sheets of plywood, though heavily scorched, had accomplished their job. The intense fire had remained confined to the area around the body. Heavy charring of the wooden floor encircled what was left of the remains. *I've got to be very careful not to step on or disturb that area in any way or leave footprints.*

He approached one of the windows and with his screwdriver, pried out a sheet of plywood. Knowing it would be very warm, he used one of the towels in each hand to carry it outside into the alley behind the barn. He did the same to the other. Now, he placed the step ladder far enough out of the way of the charring and reached over to reinstall each set of curtains back into place. The ladder was then taken into the kitchen. There, he saw an empty pail lying on the counter and pumped it full of water from the handpump. This would allow clean-up once he was finished. Pete then returned the table doily, rehung the picture back on the wall, and moved the telephone table and phone back to its original location. Now everything was just as it was before the fire. *I did it!* He happily told himself. After removing the remaining towels, taking hold of the pail of water, and the ladder, he took everything back into the barn. Once Pete was satisfied everything was out, he closed the rear door and reentered the barn.

Knowing that his clothing smelled of smoke and stink, Pete stripped down and using one of the towels, washed as clean as possible. He then inserted his dirty clothing back into the small bag and left the barn to bring up his wagon. Once back in the alley, the sheets of burnt plywood were laid scorched side down in the wagon along with the bag now containing the screwdriver. Pete raced home completely overjoyed with his success and already thinking of how he would soon be spending his newfound fortune. After returning his horse to its stall, he made his way toward the Jacks Are Wild Saloon.

Entering, he saw Hershel sitting at a table with a half-consumed bottle of whiskey and two glasses. The smile on his face was all that needed to be said. The pair drank heavily for nearly an hour before deciding it was time to start their phony fight with a few men, get arrested, and spend the night inside the jail with the perfect alibi.

Chapter 4

Sunday Morning

Tobacconist Joshua Sterling and
his wife Florence

Last night's heavy fog had nearly lifted as Joshua Sterling and his wife Florence began preparing themselves to attend morning church services. Long-time members of the First Presbyterian Church, the couple owned and operated a popular tobacco store near the town square. "It looks to be a lovely day," he said to his wife of forty-two years. "I'll go out and get Turnip Seed ready." He was referring to their aged old horse nestled comfortably inside their rear storage barn. The Sterlings had lived at their home, located on Twenty-Fourth Street, for nearly thirty years. Due to his wife's insistence, they had a telephone installed a few years ago, but Joshua drew the line on one of those silly, noisy automobiles. A horse would continue to serve their needs just fine, thank you. The couple had two grown sons, now living elsewhere with their own families.

Joshua could never understand why it took so long for a woman to dress for church. He would have Turnip Seed fed, watered, and their carriage prepared, and she still wouldn't be ready. As he stepped outside their rear kitchen doorway, he noticed the smell of burnt wood in the morning air. *Somebody must have burned some tree limbs last evening,* he thought as he entered their barn. "Good morning, old feller," he greeted the horse. Turnip Seed snorted back his form of recognition. Soon after attending to the horse's needs and hitching him to their small buggy, Joshua took hold of the bridle's cheekpiece and slowly escorted the animal out of the barn and down the driveway. Turnip Seed knew the drill well and remained stationary awaiting his master's return. Joshua detected that the burning smell was stronger at his new location as he casually glanced across the street. There, he thought he detected light smoke coming from under the home's roof soffit. Now alarmed at what he thought he saw, Joshua crossed over the street and approached his neighbor's home. The burning smell was much stronger now and the smoke a bit darker in color. *I've got to wake up Mrs. Waverly,* he told himself as he pounded frantically upon her front door. There was no answer. He pounded even louder and longer but received no reply. Joshua took hold of the doorknob. It was locked and warm to the touch. He then ran as fast as his old legs allowed and shouted inside their door, "Florence, call the telephone switchboard operator and tell her Mrs. Waverly's house is on fire!" Now, all they could do was watch and await the arrival of the Marion fire department and pray that Mrs. Waverly might be rescued in the nick of time.

As soon as the fire wagons arrived, the smell of smoke in the air caused the necessity for a charged hose line to be deployed. Two firemen, one holding an ax and another a prybar, rushed to the front door and found it locked. Though no flames had been spotted, the men hoped that their early arrival might save the structure and any occupants inside. Prying the tool against the door frame, the men got the front door open. Dark smoke and a terrible odor both men instantly recognized poured outside as they entered. One man went straight upstairs to search the second floor while the second was joined downstairs with a nozzleman. There, they were met by a terrible sight. The charred ash remains of what appeared to be a body, with only bare legs still recognizable, lay before them. New to the department, the nozzleman covered his mouth and ran outside to vomit. Soon all the home's windows were opened to ventilate the remaining smoke. There would be no successful rescue made today.

* * * * * * * * *

Outside the structure, the police positioned themselves to prevent the curious bystanders from entering. After the assistant fire chief was briefed on the grim findings, he entered the home to evaluate the situation for himself. To prevent possible destruction of the incident scene, he ordered all of his men outside and the police arrived and were notified of the fatality. They then began their initial investigation and using a neighbor's telephone, called for the photographer from the Beitler Studio, Doctor Shelby, and naturally the county coroner. The photographer lived close by and arrived quickly. He then began the task of photographing the gruesome images and the room itself from all angles. The assistant fire chief released his men to return to the station while he remained to investigate the source of the fire.

In all of his twenty-five years of service in the fire department, he had never experienced anything like this. The damage from the fire was quite easily seen, but he just couldn't fathom what he suspected might actually be the source of ignition. The intense blaze had pretty much remained confined to the heavily charred body, with burn patterns easily visible on the walls and ceiling. The table chair, pushed near the wall, suffered heavy charring, while the rocking chair to its side displayed charring on only one side. Yet the curtains above the fire showed no burn patterns, nor anything else nearby that should have been easily consumed. He then forced himself to view the horrible remains. From the feet to the knees appeared quite normal, but upward nothing remained but charred ashes. The skull had shrunk to about a third of its normal size and showed heat fracturing. The right arm was consumed, but a few fingers on the hand remained. The left arm was intact from the elbow to the fingers. It was the uncharred legs that kept returning his attention. The assistant fire chief could only draw one conclusion, as difficult as it now seemed. The fire originated on the exterior or interior of the person and consumed the body almost entirely. His early indications suggested a possibility, one that in all his years of experience he never expected to see. *It simply cannot be. There must have been combustible or flammable liquids involved here. Still, kerosene leaves a distinct odor and I cannot detect anything like it.*

Approaching the police officer in charge, he said, "Officer, I suggest you call everyone out to investigate this one."

Chapter 5

The Ghastly Scene

The Waverly dining room after the charred body was removed

Benjamin Stewart had attended church services that morning and was exiting when he noticed a police patrol wagon nearby and an officer approaching. "Top of da mornin' to ya Captain. Sorry ta be ah bothern' ya on such a lovely Sunday, but the sergeant sent me ta fetch ya. Seems we got a wee bit of a problem they need ya ta help clear up," the smiling policeman said in his foreign-born drogue.

"What is it, officer?"

"Seems someone went and burned ta death in ah house fire and I hear tell it's bloody awful ta see and smell. Tis located over on Ninth Street." Benjamin decided to wait and see everything for himself. Soon the officer had him on site and thanked him for the ride. The officer waved and drove off.

Stewart was surprised that the home did not give any indication of having been on fire. Standing outside was Police Sergeant Clark and a fire officer that he had seen before but didn't know personally. "I'm happy you're here, Captain," Clark said. "Your hotel said we might find you in church. I'm afraid we've got an unusual situation on our hands. Oh, by the way, do you two men know each other? No? Assistant Fire Chief DuPont, may I introduce Captain Stewart from the Grant County Sheriff's Department. He is our lead crime scene investigator."

The Curse of the Hanging Tree

Assistant Fire Chief Philip DuPont

"I've seen you from a distance," Benjamin said as the men shook hands. "What do we have here?"

Sergeant Clark replied, "Sir, early indications are that the victim is a Mrs. Beth Ann Waverly, age 66, a widow who has been seen living here with a man. I'm having two of our guys speak with the neighbors to see if they know who he might be."

"Captain Stewart," DuPont said, "I'll get right to the point. I have investigated many fires through the years, but I must confess that this one is quite out of the ordinary. Follow me and you can see for yourself." Though a hardened investigator, Stewart still felt himself recoiling at the sight and smell of what lay before them. DuPont continued. "As you can see, the main torso has been reduced to ashes, with the lower legs remaining, unaffected by the flames." Stewart had never seen anything like it. "The burn patterns on the walls, ceiling, and charring of the furniture point to the body as being the source of ignition," DuPont said. "If a flammable or combustible liquid was used, your people will find it during their examination. But what puzzles me is the lack of damage elsewhere." He then pointed to the curtains, the picture on the wall, the light shade over the table, and the cloth doilies. "These should have been consumed and the entire home destroyed. But as you can see, they are clean and display no damage."

"Have photographs been taken yet?"

Sergeant Clark replied that they had. "The photographer is standing by outside in case you want more taken." Stewart stooped down close to the ashen remains and scanned the burnt floor. There were no footprints in the soot or anything else to give the impression of foul play.

Doctor Walter Shelby

A known figure approached. "Captain," the medical examiner for Grant County, Doctor Shelby said. "My men are ready to remove the remains as soon as you release them." Stewart nodded and two men carefully, but with disgust showing on their faces, collected the remains and left. "I'll have my medical report ready sometime tomorrow. Feel free to call me if you have questions. This is a puzzling one, to be sure." Doctor Shelby had a long history of providing needed assistance to local law enforcement at all hours of the day or night, but enjoyed a bit of humor when it was deemed appropriate. As he was leaving, he said, "Why can't people die on normal workdays, I would like to know."

Nobody laughed at his statement but all silently agreed with it. Stewart said, "Now that the remains are gone, I want additional photos taken of the area where the body had lain. Go ahead and take as many as you can." The pale photographer who had been motioned to return inside didn't appear too happy, but complied with the order. "Expedite their development as fast as you can and have them sent straight to my office in the jail." The photographer said he would do just that.

Another policeman entered and spoke with Sergeant Clark. "We have some info on the man living here. His name is Hershel Dent. One of the neighbors said he is her brother. We'll run a check on his whereabouts shortly."

Stewart noticed the look of puzzlement on the fire officer's face and asked, "You look like you're wanting to say something."

The assistant chief nodded. "Captain, my twenty-four-hour shift ends tomorrow morning and if it's alright, I'll drop by your office sometime and see where we stand." Stewart readily agreed. DuPont then left.

Sergeant Clark commented that they had officers out looking for the missing brother. "I recognize his name. Dent is a known troublemaker." An hour later, Clark was surprised to learn that Hershel Dent was sitting comfortably in the county jail, arrested last evening for drunken brawling.

* * * * * * * * *

Later when informed of the death of his sister, Hershel Dent showed no emotion. "What do you want me to do about it?" he replied. "She drinks herself to death every day and I couldn't do anything about it. That's why I moved in, so I could help her." His statement was not believable.

"Where were you last evening?"

"I thought I would visit the Jacks Are Wild Saloon just before dark and have a couple of harmless drinks. I guess I stayed too long, got into a fight, and my friend and I were put in here." Nothing more was learned that night. There, the prisoner was to remain until his whereabouts on Saturday night could be validated. If this turned out to be a murder, he was the number one suspect in his sister's demise.

Chapter 6

The Investigation Continues

The next morning, Benjamin Stewart sat at his office desk looking over the photographs that were handed to him by his assistant, Hugo Barns. "I'm surprised you didn't call me out yesterday. I wasn't doing anything important," he informed his superior.

"I didn't feel you were needed at the time, Hugo, so you might as well enjoy your day off. Tell me, what do you make of the photos?"

The investigating assistant came around and stood looking over Benjamin's shoulder. "I know very little about fires I'm afraid. But it does strike me how a body of a woman could burn up so heavily and not set the entire house ablaze."

There was a light knock on his door as both officers looked up. "Here's the medical report from the doctor, sir," an aide said as he handed it over.

After reading through the report, Benjamin laid it down. "No sign of any foreign flammable or combustible liquids were found, though traces of fat residue were noted." He then looked out the window and thought upon the report's findings. "We have her brother and his friend incarcerated, but before releasing them, I want you to contact the bartender that worked Saturday evening at the Jacks Are Wild Saloon. After working the late-night shift, he's probably at home. Ask him if he remembers Hershel Dent and his partner being there, and if so, when? Find out anything you can and report back to me over at the Waverly home." Hugo left and was out in the hallway when he was stopped for information by a visitor.

"Hello. I'm looking for the office of Captain Stewart."

"Two doors down on the left," Hugo said. The man thanked him and entered the office. It was off-duty Assistant Fire Chief DuPont.

"Captain, is this an inconvenient time for me to drop by and speak with you?"

"Not at all, please have a chair," Steward replied. "I was just looking over the photographs from the fire and trying to make heads or tails out of the chemical analysis findings we just received. There is no indication of flammable or combustible liquids, just traces of fat residue."

"I feared that to be the case. Would you mind if I ask you a couple of questions?" DuPont asked. "I don't want to be perceived as butting into your investigation though."

"No, go right ahead. What's on your mind?"

"Let me venture a guess as to the lady's general description. An older woman, overweight, alcoholic, smoker, possibly suffering from depression or diabetes."

"From what the officers learned from questioning her neighbors, I would say you are probably right on most of what you asked. As for her medical condition…"

"Captain, I hope you won't think me crazy for asking you this, but are you familiar with the term spontaneous human combustion?"

A surprised look appeared upon Benjamin Stewart's face. "I've heard the term before. Why? Is that what we're dealing with here?"

"I'm just not quite sure yet. I gave a class to my shift a couple of months ago on the subject. I brought along my notes from the research I did and additional information from a medical booklet I used entitled: The Anatomy of Drunkenness by Robert Macnish. I brought it along for you to review later if you desire. In all, there are thirty documented cases of spontaneous human combustion from the sixteenth century up to the present. It appears they all have the same three basic chrematistics:

1. The surroundings from the fire are not overly damaged.
2. No visible fire sources can be found.
3. Some parts of the body are left fully intact.

All the cases were reported to burn from the victim's inside out, reducing the area involved to ashes while remaining parts of the body go untouched."

Benjamin Stewart picked up the offered book and opened its cover. "I see it's a public handout, courtesy of the Ladies Temperance Society."

DuPont smiled. "Yes, they use it to scare heavy drinkers into thinking they might suddenly burst into flames, but the individual cases published in that booklet are based on documented historical circumstances."

"But I've read that the human body is composed of seventy percent water. If so, then how can a body burn itself to ashes?" Steward asked.

"Our bodies are also composed of fat and methane gas, with the obese having extra-large accumulations. That's why I asked about the victim being overweight. The theory is that something we don't understand at the moment, most likely at the molecular level, somehow starts a chain reaction that ignites the body fat and tissues into burning. Nearly all those mentioned in the booklet have the same classic profile I mentioned."

"The medical examiner's report does say that excessive fat residue was found within the ashes, but I'm not ready yet to write this off as spontaneous human combustion. I was planning on going back to the home and spending more time looking around. Care to join me? My automobile is setting outside."

"I noticed it when I arrived. Thanks for the offer. Yes, please, lead the way."

Once outside, DuPont offered to crank the car. "It's a real beauty. I wish the powers-that-be would allow us to purchase a motorized fire engine. It's hard to change the minds of some of the old-timers who don't like modern ways, I'm afraid." Once outside the home, entry was easy as Benjamin Stewart still possessed the front door key.

"Let's open all the curtains and windows and air this place out a bit first," Benjamin said. Once completed, the men stepped back outside to hopefully allow the remaining terrible smell to clear. Stewart indicated he was going to look around outside and left DuPont standing on the front porch. Only a couple of minutes had passed when a man approached the house. It was the officer who gave DuPont the directions for Stewart's office.

"If you're looking for Captain Stewart, he went around back somewhere."

"Thanks," the investigating assistant replied and walked toward the rear of the home. He saw the open barn door and entered to see Benjamin Stewart feeding and watering a famished old horse. "I spoke with the bartender, sir. He said that he remembered Hershel Dent arriving very early in the evening very distinctly because Dent sat at a small table for two all alone with a bottle of whiskey and two glasses. A couple of men tried to join him but were apparently denied. He said that later things were getting busy and he hadn't noticed more until another man arrived. It was Pickpocket Pete Hampton, who had experienced run-ins with the bartender in the past. Later, he said that his eyes were drawn to the sudden movement and shouting by Hampton, who lunged toward the back of two men sitting next to them. Then a brawl broke out and eventually Hampton and Dent were arrested. Afterward, the other two men involved said they had no idea why the fight had broken out and claimed they hadn't even spoken with the pair all evening."

Stewart mentally filed away the information. He then proceeded to search the barn, paying close attention to the step ladder. "Let's go inside the house now." Hugo was then introduced to the assistant fire chief.

"Are you familiar with the typical V pattern displayed on burnt walls?" DuPont asked. "As you can see, we have heavy scorching here, there, and on the ceiling, but no real V pattern. Very strange." He then got down and looked at the bottom of the chair that sat next to the wall. There was a heavy charring present on the legs and bottom of the seat. DuPont then moved the chair away from the wall to reveal no scorch mark. "This chair sat here during the fire. I'm guessing the woman was sitting here when the fire broke out until she tumbled to the floor."

Stewart shook his head. "I see two flaws in your theory. First, ask yourself why a very heavy woman would choose to sit here against the wall in a hard table chair, presumably drinking herself unconsciousness, when a larger, far more comfortable rocking chair sat unused beside her? Remember, we found a near-empty bottle of whiskey and a used glass sitting side-by-side on the kitchen counter. Would anyone in her condition go to that extent of neatness or would she have sat the bottle and glass on this drum table or the floor itself? No, I feel someone has moved them for her. Second, I need Hugo to demonstrate something for us. Would you mind pulling one of those clean table chairs over here out of the way? Thanks, please have a seat, my friend." Hugo did so. "Now pretended you are becoming unconscious and fall out of the chair for us." The assistant did so. "Now try it again but attempt to catch yourself with an arm." After several attempts, the demonstration ended.

"Did any of Hugo's movements resemble in any way how Mrs. Waverly's body was lain out on her back, so neat and proper? There simply isn't any way that would happen, unless she lowered herself into that position and went to sleep. No gentlemen, we have a murder on our hands. Someone has gone to great lengths to make us think this is a case of spontaneous human combustion. While I was out in the barn, I discovered and picked up the small step ladder. I found two small smudge marks on the bottom of the top step, most likely from being carried by someone with soot on their fingers."

"Then our assailant must have obtained a large amount of liquified fat and dumped it on the body to produce the heavy combustion," DuPont said. "Someone used the step ladder to cover the windows, remove the curtains, and relocate everything else just to throw us off track. I bet our arsonist-murderer has read Macnish's book!"

"Somehow, Dent's friend Pete Hampton must fit into all of this. I bet he was the one who started the fire, then went to join Dent at the saloon to establish their alibi," Hugo Barns suggested.

"I was about to suggest the same thing," Stewart said. "Let's go check Hampton's residence. I have a feeling we'll find what we're looking for inside his barn."

"Then I'll let you gentlemen tend to your policing matters. Thank you for clearing up my spontaneous human combustion theory. You've saved me a ton of embarrassment," DuPont said. "I live close by and can use the walk to help clear my mind. Good luck in your investigation, gentlemen."

* * * * * * * * *

After arriving at Hampton's rented residence, Stewart and Barns found another hungry horse, but there was nothing there to feed it. "Once we're finished here, I'll see if a neighbor can come by and care for his horse temporarily," Hugo said. A wagon sat outside the barn and just as they approached, the stench from the fire was easily detected. There inside the footboard of the wagon, was a small bag containing soiled clothing. Inside the wagon were two sheets of plywood. Stewart flipped one over to reveal the heavy fire scorching.

"Forget your idea of contacting a neighbor, Hugo. Hitch up the horse and take all this in as evidence. Then make arrangements with one of the stables to care for his and Dent's horse. Their owners will probably be behind bars for the rest of their lives anyway."

Over inside the Grant County jail, Pickpocket Pete Hampton and Hershel Dent were awaiting being brought before a judge, expecting to pay a small fine for brawling, and then be released. Instead, each was soon brought into separate rooms and heavily questioned. Pete Hampton was questioned first and denied any knowledge of the death of Mrs. Waverly, or the fire. Then Captain Steward informed him of the evidence collected and that he would be charged with first-degree murder. Suddenly the thought of hanging for a murder he didn't commit overcame him, and Pickpocket Pete Hampton began singing like a bird. With his full confession in hand, Stewart presented the information to Hershel Dent, who displayed no emotion and refused to talk, but knew then that his days of freedom were behind him.

Both were later charged and went to trial in Grant County Circuit Court One. Each man claimed his innocence, but the

The Curse of the Hanging Tree

evidence presented to the jury was overwhelming. On Friday, November 26th, 1905, both prisoners were hanged at the Indiana State Prison in Michigan City. The home, properties, and money of Mrs. Beth Ann Waverly found their way into the possession of her very surprised cousin living in Kokomo.

THE SCORPION

The Curse of the Hanging Tree

Returning Cast of Characters

Captain Benjamin Stewart	Crime Scene Investigator
Hugo Barns	Investigator's Assistant
Sergeant Clark	Marion Policeman
Joshua Sterling	Tobacconist
Florence Sterling	Wife

New Cast of Characters

Chad McCormick	Owner of McCormick's Power & Light
Lawrence Fields	Company Office Manager
Lisa McCormick	Wife/English Teacher at Horace Mann H.S.
Victor Stanton	Vice Principal at Horace Mann H.S.
Barnaby Andrews	Science and Biology Teacher
Brian O'Brian	New Marion Fireman

Alan E. Losure

View Looking South from Third Street, Marion, Indiana

Chapter 1

Tuesday, April 10, 1906

Horace Mann High School, Marion, Indiana

Named after the famous public education reformer Horace Mann, this elegant high school, located between Third and Fourth Street, proved Marion's commitment to furthering their children's education. Equipped with a multitude of classrooms, a spacious library, a large study hall, various offices, and a basement coal-fired heating system, this beautiful structure was the perceived envy of most towns, and was widely considered to stand the test of time for countless future generations of students.

* * * * * * * * *

Vice Principal Victor Stanton

Vice Principal Victor Stanton had one immediate goal in life; to become the next principal at Horace Mann High School and replace the old man, Edward Cassidy, currently holding that title. Feared by his students and mostly avoided by the school staff, Stanton tended to be an authoritarian, much like his grandfather, Edward Stanton, the Secretary of War under the Lincoln Administration. He demanded much from his students and had no hesitation in handling disciplinary issues when they arose. Just ask the many troublesome boys, and yes, a few girls, who met with his wooden paddle or experienced school expulsion. The faculty members tended to refer to each other by their first name while in a private setting away from students, but never to Mr. Stanton, who seemed to enjoy that figure of authority. Even Principal Cassidy feared Stanton and allowed his much younger colleagues a free hand in managing the staff, dealing with parents, and enforcing school safety procedures. Stanton had come quickly through the ranks, starting as a history teacher before assuming his current position. When the need arose for Stanton to fill in for a missing or sick teacher, one could always assume there to be near-perfect class attention and cooperation from all the students. If not…well, he had a firm grasp of any given situation.

Very little was known about the man outside of work. He had no family photos on his desk or walls and never spoke about himself or where he came from to anybody. The teachers had a lounge where they could relax between classes, but Stanton never entered the room or ever attempted to socialize with the workforce. His meals, consisting of simple fruit or a sandwich, were always consumed at his desk behind a closed office door.

* * * * * * * * *

Teacher Barnaby Andrews

    If a poll was taken from the student body, as well as the faculty members, the most popular teacher by far would be science and biology teacher Barnaby Andrews. Impeccably dressed with an outgoing personality and a smile on his face, Barney, as his many friends called him, was a joy to work with. He stood at six feet and weighed in at 170 pounds. Barney made the study of science and biology interesting to his students, rather than simply teaching dry scientific facts, and had no difficulty in filling his classroom. He was single and was presumed to have no difficulty in finding opportunities to spend time with the ladies. Barney came to Marion from the state of Illinois and he seemed most satisfied with his present working situation. Little beyond this was known about the man, and many assumed he possessed a bit of money as he was thought to live in one of the upper-class boarding houses in town.

Barney was often seen working in the school's science lab after school ended, conducting some sort of unknown scientific experiments. Inside a locked storage cabinet in his classroom, Barney kept a personal array of chemicals and a high-powered microscope, vastly superior to the school-issued instrument used by his students.

* * * * * * * * *

Chad & Lisa McCormick

Another hectic day had finally ended at the high school as Mrs. Lisa McCormick collected her thoughts and her homework to board the streetcar home. She and her husband had recently purchased a modest home on the south side of Marion. Originally from Marion, Lisa had met her future husband at a college baseball game and began dating during her last year of studies at Normal College. Lisa had always dreamed of being an English teacher and was thrilled at being accepted at her old school. Due to her youthful appearance and charming good looks, she often felt herself being openly flirted with by some of the older boys in her classroom. This she skillfully handled by resolving everything without inflicting embarrassment to the student. Mrs. McCormick was a well-liked and respected teaching staff member who saw nothing but a bright future ahead.

Her husband Chad was originally from Arizona but became disgruntled with the hot, dry summer conditions and sought a milder climate in which to live. One of his friends growing up had originally come from Indiana and the idea of four distinct seasons sounded appealing to Chad. His father had been a very successful engineer in Arizona and had hoped his son would follow in his footprints, but this hadn't happened. Instead, Chad moved to Indiana and found a job working as a teller at Marion National Bank. The odd name of "teller" originated from an old English word meaning, "to count." Chad found his new occupation to be easy work. With the funds his parents had given to him, he found himself living most comfortably in a boarding house where his meals were provided by a kindly old woman. Then one Saturday afternoon, he met Miss Lisa Billings who was in her senior year in college. Their courtship moved at a pleasant pace until one day, a tragic telegram arrived, informing him that both his parents had been killed in a railcar derailment. Chad returned alone to Arizona for the funeral. Soon his parent's assets were made available to him and he found himself a wealthy young man. After returning to Marion, he found that his old job had been filled during his absence. This came as a relief to him as he was already planning his future. Chad determined it best to remain at the boarding house for the time being, as he was uncertain where his involvement with Miss Billings might lead, but it now appeared more promising.

One day he learned that a small local electrical company was for sale. Chad already possessed an overall understanding of the workings of electricity, having learned the basics from his engineer father. The installation of home and business electrical lighting was becoming quite popular with the wealthier clientele. Chad could see himself purchasing the existing business and expanding electricity to even moderate homeowners. With three electricians already on hand and an office manager anxious to keep his job, the only major change needed was the new owner's name on the sign. Looking deeper into the present owner's reason for wishing to sell, Chad learned that the elderly man had cancer and was looking to liquidate his assets while he still could. A low-ball offer was submitted by Chad, which was immediately rejected, but a reasonable counter-offer was then made. Chad jumped upon it and the purchase was complete. Soon a new sign hung outside the building that read: *McCormick's Power & Light.*

Last summer, with his new business flourishing, Chad McCormick proposed marriage to Miss Lisa Billings. The young woman accepted and the happy couple honeymooned at Niagara Falls before returning to Marion and purchasing a lovely new home. With the start of another new school year, the English class teacher now had a new name: Mrs. McCormick.

* * * * * * * * *

Lawrence Fields, Office Manager

Lawrence Fields remained a very angry man. Last year, he had silently begun planning to make an offer to the old owner in purchasing the electrical company. Larry, as he preferred to be called, hadn't been in any hurry to make the offer, thinking that the longer he waited, and the sicker the old man got, the cheaper he might make the purchase. And then it happened. Out of nowhere, an offer was presented by a stranger and before Larry knew of it, an agreement had been reached. Larry felt sucker-punched by the news. On that day he and the company's three electricians finally met the new owner, Larry had a hard time not laughing out loud. This Chad McCormick looked like a kid, a little rich kid to boot! The next few days had been a blur to office manager Lawrence Fields. "The rich kid," as Larry referred to him, acted like he understood the electronics business and began to make subtle changes. One in particular riled up Larry. The old owner had awarded a five percent bonus for any new contracts that Larry managed to sign up. That policy had now ended. Larry felt his years of service and experience were now being ignored, and he was now thought of simply as one of the workers. Every day he told himself that he should quit and return home to Muncie, but he held off making that decision. *There are ways to make this company fail, and when it does, I will swoop in and purchase it for pennies on the dollar!* The only thing that Larry Fields admired about Chad McCormick, was his pretty young wife, Lisa.

Chapter 2

The Letter

Several days soon passed. Chad McCormick tended to return home for lunch while his wife remained at school. He was overall relatively pleased with the expansion of his new business, having secured two new home electrical installation projects and one small business. He had also run several advertisements in the Marion Chronicle and Leader newspapers advertising his company. He hadn't managed to resolve the internal friction he felt by his three electricians. Sure, they smiled when he spoke to them, but Chad could feel the tension in the air and wondered if any might quit. The main problem he felt was his office manager, Lawrence Fields. All of his attempts to improve whatever issue existed between them seemed to have failed. Chad could only surmise that Fields resented him. No doubt the argument they had about a commission on new sales had set them on a collision course. *Maybe I should give in and reinstate that old policy? Maybe doing so might change things for the better? I just fear giving in at this point and setting the wrong example. After all, I am the boss, not him.*

Returning home for lunch, Chad glanced inside their mailbox and extracted three letters. Without paying any further attention to them, he made a sandwich and poured a glass of water from the kitchen pump. After finishing his lunch, he casually picked up the letters and opened the first. It was from an old friend in Arizona that corresponded occasionally. The second was an advertisement from an insurance company. It was the third that quickly caught Chad's attention. It read:

> Tis thee, my dear, that I adore
> And will, my dear, forevermore.
> Same time and place.

Chad was shocked by what he just read and saw that the envelope had been addressed to his wife Lisa. Great anger and jealousy swept through his body as the true meaning of the words could not be any plainer. *My wife is cheating on me!* Chad stuffed the letter back into its envelope, then inserted it in his jacket's pocket. *This is one love letter that Lisa won't receive!* His mind raced ahead, considering all of the male names she had casually mentioned from school and any neighbors or friends. After mentally reviewing all of the possibilities he could come up with, one man stood out above all others: The science teacher, Barney Andrews. *Of course, it could be someone I don't know, so I'll have to play this close to the vest until I am sure. And when I do, then it's game on!*

* * * * * * * * *

Joshua and Florence Sterling

Across town at Sterling's Tobacco Shop, Florence was quite happy with the mid-afternoon lull in customers. Being on her feet all day made her legs tired and sore. Her husband Joshua, however, didn't seem at all bothered by the long hours required to run their shop. She often wondered where he got his energy. Florence was in favor of selling the shop and enjoying retirement, but Joshua would have nothing to do with it. *I'll be here working until the day I die…and perhaps even later*, he joked. Knowing her husband as well as she did, she wouldn't put anything past him.

Joshua was in the backroom obtaining new stock for the empty spots on the shelves when he heard their telephone ring. As he re-entered, he heard Florence taking down an order. As she hung up. "That was Fire Station Number One. They placed this order," she said as she handed the list to him. The old man broke into another one of his silly grins. Truth be told, Joshua always behaved that way when he took an order down to the boys at the fire station. You see, he had worked for many years as a fireman and loved the opportunity to chew the fat with them. Joshua gathered up the various tobaccos and left on foot to make the deliveries.

"I may be a while, Mother. The boys just love to hear my exciting tales of saving lives and protecting personal property, and they keep begging me to stay a little longer."

Florence simply shook her head and started sweeping up the floor. *That old windbag would still be riding the hose wagon if they would allow it!*

Fire Station Number One

Joshua arrived at the fire station and was met by his happy customers to complete their tobacco purchases. One of his customers was an unfamiliar face. "I don't think I've met you before, young man," Joshua said.

"I'm somewhat new to the Marion fire department, sir. My name is Brian O'Brian"

The old man chuckled, but before he could reply, the younger man continued.

"I know...I know. I hear it all the time. You see, I was named after my grandfather who immigrated from the old country."

Joshua held out his hand. "It's a pleasure to meet you, Brian O'Brian. You're in good company here, I might add." Joshua turned and looked toward the stove. "Coffee?" One of the men poured their visitor a cup and the group sat down at a small table.

The Curse of the Hanging Tree

One of the firemen spoke. "Brian, Joshua here is one of our original firemen here in the city."

The young man's opinion of the old man rose significantly with this knowledge. "I bet you've seen a lot in your day," Brian replied. The other firemen quickly glanced at their fellows, knowing full well that Joshua was about to start reciting stories of the old days once again.

"Yes, as a matter of fact, I've seen a lot." He took a sip of his coffee, then continued. "I remember I was one of the first twenty men who volunteered to serve back in '53. You see, to provide fire coverage for your home or business back then, you had to become a paying member of an association. I believe it cost fifty cents to join. If any type of bell was handy, it was rung to indicate a fire. If not, runners came to the home of the volunteers. Then in '83, the fire department was re-organized and a fire station was built behind what was then the old Presbyterian church. We received seventy-five cents an hour for active service and our apparatus was a large wagon containing buckets that we pulled by a rope. That's where the term bucket brigade comes from." Joshua paused to take another sip.

"You see, one day we responded to a fire and were pulling the apparatus when Jack Butler, who was the manager of the livery stable, rode past us and we threw him the rope. After that, he volunteered to pull it. That's about the time my wife insisted I was a bit too old to fight fires, but I kept up to date on what was happening. Soon after, they began to use a team of horses to pull the apparatus. The horses' names were Pete and Prince. Fine animals too. One of the strangest fires I saw was when the First National Bank burned in '76. They had to carry all the money out in buckets and assembled everything under guard on the courthouse lawn. Yes, Brian O'Brian, you are indeed in fine company with this bunch!" Joshua finished his coffee and was preparing to leave. "I guess I better be heading back to the shop now before the wife sends the police to get me," he joked.

"I was wondering, do you think we'll ever have a motorized apparatus here?" Brian asked.

Joshua made a sour face at that question. "Why in God's name would they want to go and do such a stupid thing as that!" With a wave, Joshua Sterling left to return to the tobacco shop

* * * * * * * * *

An uncomfortable stillness filled the air of the McCormick home that Lisa picked up on. Despite her efforts, Chad seemed distant and cold, while refusing to say what was bothering him. The following evening, she had entered the room she was using for an office and found him going through her to-be-graded school homework. When asked what he was looking for, Chad gave a generic reply that didn't make any sense. Later he stated he was going to a lodge meeting that night and would be home around ten o'clock. Chad grabbed his hat and left, but instead of heading to the lodge, he found a secluded spot and watched the front door of their home to see if she left. If so, he would follow her and find out who she was seeing.

Lisa thought it quite odd as she didn't know her husband was involved in any lodge, but looked forward to a few hours of peace and quiet. *Work must be troubling him*, she thought. Later he returned home and went straight to bed without saying anything. As he lay there, his mind was racing non-stop. *Maybe she went out the back door to meet up with her lover... or maybe they spoke on the telephone?* Chad was determined to discover who the man was once and for all no matter how long it took.

The following morning, after many hours of restless sleep, Chad felt he knew who his wife's lover was. They were sitting down at the breakfast table and Lisa attempted to strike up a conversation to hopefully clear the air. "How was your lodge meeting, sweetheart?"

He stopped eating and gave her a hateful stare. "I know who you're carrying on with behind my back. It's that no-good science teacher, Barnaby Andrews. You might as well admit it, Lisa. I intercepted one of the love poems he sent here a few days ago!"

Lisa about choked on her coffee. "What?...What are you saying? I'm not having an affair with Barney Andrews!" The room exploded with shouting and accusations. Finally, Lisa finished dressing for school and slammed the door on her way out of their home. Chad sat there drinking another cup of coffee as he considered what to do next.

CHAPTER 3

May 2, 1906

Science teacher Barnaby Andrews remained after-hours in the school's chemistry lab, lost in his work and oblivious to the hours that had passed since school had let out. Today's research was in the study of the four types of human blood groups: Types O, A, B, and AB only discovered five years before. The school janitor had poked his head in only moments before to say that he would be mopping the hallway and to be careful when leaving. Barney acknowledged him and realized it was a hint for him to finish up and leave for the day. There would be ample time tomorrow evening before darkness set in to return to his studies. He was in the process of carrying back his personally owned microscope to the storage area when the window in front of him shattered in broken glass particles. Upon hearing the terrible noise, the janitor rushed back into the science lab as both men stared at the visible bullet hole in the shattered window.

* * * * * * * * *

The following morning before the start of school, the incident was reported by the janitor to Vice Principal Stanton, who immediately left to survey the window for himself. Inside the classroom, preparing for the start of class, was Barney Andrews. As soon as the vice principal entered, Barney knew that the janitor had reported the incident. "Tell me exactly what happened last evening," the man demanded to know. After hearing the brief story, Stanton asked if he had any idea who or why someone would take a shot at him.

"No, I am completely baffled by this, but perhaps it was some type of sick joke orchestrated by one of the students."

"Attempted murder is no joke, Mr. Andrews," a visibly angry Stanton replied. "I want this room sealed off today. I'm informing the police of the incident so keep everyone else away. Send all your students to the study hall today." Soon word of the incident quickly spread to the entire student body and staff.

* * * * * * * * *

"Looks like a 44-40 slug," Marion Police Sergeant Clark replied after using his penknife to extract the bullet from the rear wall. The other officer nodded. Clark then approached the science teacher. "Have you arrived at anyone who might be holding a grudge against you? Perhaps a student you failed or had harsh words with? What about your social life, any issues there?" Clark asked.

"No, sir. I can't think of anyone who might wish me harm," the now visibly troubled man said.

"Why were you here after-hours anyway?"

"I often stay late to continue my laboratory studies. The school is wonderful in allowing me this opportunity to continue my research," Barney said.

"I suggest you end that practice, at least for a while," Clark offered. "It might be best to stay in crowds and leave right after school ends."

"I agree with that assessment, Mr. Andrews," the vice-principal said. A disappointed Barnaby Andrews knew that both men were right. "I am now deeply concerned with the safety of our children, as well as our staff. Should police officers be stationed outside the school?" Stanton asked.

"I don't feel that is necessary at this point. Here's my business card, Mr. Andrews. Please let me know if you have any later thoughts about who our perpetrator might be. I need leads, no matter how insignificant they may seem to you. Good day, gentlemen."

Victor Stanton turned and said, "Mr. Andrews, take the rest of today to compose yourself. Your normal classes shall begin again tomorrow. I'll instruct the janitor to replace the window."

It seemed very strange for Barnaby Andrews to leave the school during teaching hours. Instead of returning immediately to his boarding house, he walked the downtown streets of the town in deep thought.

The next day a letter without a return address was shoved under the front door of the boarding house and discovered by the landlady. It was addressed to Barnaby Andrews. Thinking little about it, she laid it next to his plate at the supper table. Knowledge of the shooting incident had spread to the men and women living there, but each had refrained from discussing it with Barney. All eyes watched as he opened the envelope to read its contents. It appeared to many that the color on his face turned pale as its true meaning registered in his mind. Grabbing up the envelope, and with the letter in hand, Barney excused himself from the table and climbed the stairs to his room. Upon entering, Barney sat upon his bed and stared at what was written. Its message couldn't be clearer.

*Next time I won't miss.
The Scorpion*

* * * * * * * * *

The following morning, Barnaby Andrews called the phone number on Sergeant Clark's card and explained what had occurred. The letter and envelope were then picked up by another policeman and taken to Sergeant Clark for examination.

Chapter 4

Captain Stewart's Involvement

Benjamin Stewart was sitting in his office, located within the jail, when a soft knock upon the door caught his attention. Looking up he saw the familiar face of Sergeant Clark. "Can I bother you for a moment, Captain?" the Marion policeman said.

"Sure, Clark. What's up?"

"You're familiar with the high school shooting this week, right?"

Stewart replied he had read the report.

"Well sir, this was shoved under the door of the boarding house where the intended victim lives. I obtained it only this morning from him." Clark handed it over to his friend.

Stewart studied the envelope carefully. "Just a plain ordinary unmailed envelope," he said. "Printed to disguise the handwriting, most likely." He then opened the letter. "Again, an ordinary paper you can buy in any department store." Stewart concentrated upon the printed words. "The threat appears real. Tell me again about the man."

"His name is Barnaby Andrews, the science and biology teacher. I spoke with the vice principal privately and he tells me Andrews is will-liked by the student and teachers. He feels the shot came from someone not directly connected with the school. My superior has decided to have a plainclothesman keep an eye on him, but my gut tells me that won't be enough. A man with a high-powered rifle could strike from almost anywhere. I was hoping you might have a different idea. I can assure you, Mr. Andrews seems quite shaken up about receiving that written threat."

"Where does he live?"

"In Keller's Boarding House over on Third Street. I hear it's a real nice place."

"I would suggest you interview everyone who lives there. Maybe someone is holding a grudge against him or perhaps they may have seen or heard something that might help provide a clue. In the meantime, I'll have Hugo go through our files for known shooters. Maybe we'll get lucky and find a connection." Sergeant Clark left the jail hoping that their efforts might just be enough.

Later that evening at the boarding house's supper table, the other occupants started complaining about being interviewed by the police. Finally, the owner, the elderly Mrs. Keller ended the conversation by saying, "If I wished our Mr. Andrews harm, I would ask him to marry me!" Everyone at the table laughed except Barnaby Andrews who sat eating his soup in silence.

* * * * * * * * *

By mid-morning the following day, Chad McCormick had already received three complaint telephone calls from his customers of workers not showing up as scheduled. Chad had had enough and called Lawrence Fields into his office. "Close the door behind you," the young owner demanded. "Fields, I am sick and tired of receiving complaints from our customers about our workmen. Either they don't show up on the job site or leave for a couple of hours. One customer claimed he smelled alcohol on the breath of one of the returning men. I won't tolerate that kind of behavior! You are the office manager. I expect you to knock a few heads together and stop this foolishness or I'll fire you and run everything myself. Do you understand me?"

Fields turned red in the face and Chad could tell he was fighting the urge to explode in anger. "Sir," he said through gritted teeth, "you don't understand the business."

"I understand when someone is GIVING ME the business! I want it stopped immediately, or I'll fire the entire bunch of you! Now get out and tell those three their job is on the line and to straighten out…or else!" Fields slammed the door on his way out.

As if he didn't have enough on his mind already. Trying to catch his cheating wife with that dirtbag schoolteacher was encompassing his every thought. Now his electrical business was failing. He needed to clear his mind and concentrate. His home life was terrible. They were either fighting or giving each other the silent treatment. For several weeks now they had slept in different bedrooms. He had been so happy during that first year of their marriage. Now he was considering hiring a private investigator to produce the legal proof he would need for a divorce on a charge of adultery, and only one man was to blame: Barnaby Andrews. Chad's mind raced in every direction in determining what to do next.

The days passed by...

Only one more week of schooling remained for the students at Horace Man High School. The only person who didn't seem happy was Barney Andrews. His previous friendly, outgoing personality now seemed a thing of the past as he moved about silently, saying very little to anyone. Instead of teaching science in a way that excited students, he now instructed them to read a chapter and prepare for the next day's test. Students felt dread at having to attend his class and many felt sorry for the poor man. He seemed almost paranoid. One day a student dropped a small test tube onto the floor, shattering it into a million pieces, and Mr. Andrews was seen diving for cover before composing himself. By the end of the day, every student in the school had heard the story. What nobody knew was that another threatening letter had been mailed and delivered the evening before. That morning, it had been turned over to the police department. It read:

In the coming days ahead,
You, dear Romeo,
Shall soon be dead!
The Scorpion

CHAPTER 5

A discovery is made

Chad made it a point to look through his wife's possessions whenever she was absent, which was becoming more and more often. To be honest, there were times in which he told himself that perhaps he was mistaken, and maybe he should accept her claims of innocence. What man wouldn't have doubt when it concerned the woman he still loves? One evening, he saw Lisa heating water for her bath and resolved to inspect her dressing table once she entered the bathtub. Soon he had his chance and could hear his wife lightly singing to herself. It didn't take long until he discovered the evidence. Tucked away inside her handbag, Chad discovered a gold necklace he didn't remember seeing. It had a small locket attached to it. Opening the locket, he saw one word engraved upon it. *Forever.*

Without thinking, he burst through the bathroom door and shouted, "Lisa, who gave you this forever locket? Don't lie to me!"

In a calm voice, she replied, "My parents gave it to me years ago when I graduated from high school. I discovered it yesterday when I went through an old box. Why must you distrust me? Are you deliberately trying to destroy our marriage!" Chad then brought up again the mailed love poem. An angry look appeared on her face. "It was probably just a student prank, for God's sake!" Their fighting continued. That evening, Chad made mental plans to look for a private detective once and for all. And then a new idea entered his mind where no private investigator would be needed after all. One that would strike a painful message to Lisa and her lover. *I'm going to burn down that blasted school and put the blame right on Andrews. That will fix them both and the juicy scandal will haunt each of them for the rest of their miserable lives!*

The following early afternoon, Chad left work and waited outside of the high school until everyone had left. He then crept toward the main door, opened it, looked inside, and listened. He saw and heard nobody. Knowing the location of the first-floor science lab, Chad entered the building and made his way inside. Looking about, he saw just what he was after; a white lab coat hanging on a peg close to Andrew's desk. Just to make sure, he removed it and glanced inside at the label. Andrew's name was written across the label. Overjoyed with his good luck, but fearful of discovery, Chad rolled up the coat and left the building. He then returned to the rear of his office building and hid the coat inside a wooden box in the alley. He then entered to wait until everyone had left for the day. Chad then approached the office typewriter, inserted a single sheet of paper under the roller, and tapped out his intended message using only his index fingers. Finally satisfied, he signed a name to the bottom. Reading over it, Chad smiled. This was what he typed out:

> Barney,
>
> I must break off our affair as I have decided to remain with my husband and make a go of our marriage. Chad is a wonderful man and somehow, I had forgotten it in my lust for you. This is all my fault and I can only blame myself for allowing it to happen. Please do not attempt to speak with me at school.
>
> *Lisa*

Chad then folded the letter into thirds, as if it had been mailed, and inserted it into the vest pocket of the white lab coat. With the box in hand, Chad made his way home and placed it inside his rear shed. Now all he had to do was wait for darkness. *Then the fun will begin!*

Another evening meal was consumed in silence as the couple no longer even bothered to look at each other. Knowing that her husband tended to leave after supper, Lisa washed up the dirty dishes and entered her room for the night.

* * * * * * * * *

Outside, Chad entered his shed and, using the fading sunlight, inventoried exactly what he would need to carry out his mission. He had two one-gallon containers of kerosene he used to clean paintbrushes with, one of which had been slightly used. Chad dawned some leather gloves and using a clean rag, wiped away any lingering fingerprints. These were then inserted into the box and covered with the lab coat. He then placed the leather gloves, his old coveralls, and a screwdriver inside. Everything was now ready as he waited for additional hours to pass. With the high school relatively close by, he won't have much of a walk to accomplish. Since most people would be in for the night, Chad didn't expect to be seen but would take appropriate measures to remain in the shadows. Shortly after ten o'clock, he picked up the wooden box and made his way toward his intended target.

As Chad approached the massive school, he made his way to the rear of the building and stopped in front of the coal chute. This was how coal wagons delivered the combustibles to heat a large basement boiler. Once the water turned to steam, it provided heat to the many classroom registers. With winter now a distant memory, Chad expected to find a greatly diminished pile of coal awaiting him. He approached one of the small glass windows and attempted to see inside. It was pitch black and offered no view. This window would have to be broken for him to enter. He removed all of his equipment from the box and stepped into the coveralls. Chad then put on the pair of gloves and grabbed the lab coat and the screwdriver. The lab coat would be used to help muffle the sound of the shattering of the glass and to prevent himself from being cut by its sharp edges. Using the wooden handle as a battering ram, Chad swung it against the glass. Nothing happened. He tried again and again until the glass finally gave way. Now he removed as many pieces as he could and discarded them inside. Then, with the metal edge of the screwdriver, he attempted to smooth out the bottom wooden frame still containing glass. Finally, he was satisfied. He then draped the coat over the bottom of the window frame to protect him from what little remained.

Chad had naturally never stood in the basement of the high school before and wondered how far a drop he would have to make. After wedging himself inside the window frame, he dropped to the concrete floor. The fall inside was deeper than he expected, more like eight feet or more. After picking himself up, Chad lit a match and looked about. There beside him were the remains of the winter's coal pile. This was exactly what he had hoped to find. Now it was time to look for the janitor storage room in search of a wooden step ladder. He quickly found one. On a shelf above the janitor's work table sat an oil lamp. It was brought into position and lit. Now he could see much better. Chad then moved the ladder into position under the open window, climbed up its steps, and obtained the two cans of kerosene along with the screwdriver. The lab coat was placed outside the window for safekeeping. Using great care, he poured the contents of the opened can onto the coal pile. Then the lid was punctured on the other and used the same way. Chad placed both empty containers back outside and made his way out the window. Now very satisfied with his work, he removed the gloves, stripped off the dirty coveralls, and threw them and the wooden box inside the window onto the coal pile. Chad wanted everything to look like Andrews discarded the cans and lab coat, so he made sure that they were far enough away so as not to be consumed by the blaze, but easily discovered by the police later on. Feeling all was now ready, he returned to the open window, lit a match, and dropped it onto the coal pile. The first match bounced off and didn't ignite, but the second did. A loud whoosh emitted with a bright flame. He ran into the darkness and stopped about a block away. Flames were shooting out of the window along with heavy dark smoke. Chad McCormick returned home a very satisfied man.

* * * * * * * * *

Across town, office manager Lawrence Fields was reflecting upon his boss's strange temperament. *It's as if he's already given up on the business. At this rate, I'll soon own it and start things rolling.*

* * * * * * * * *

Benjamin Stewart was preparing for bed when he heard many loud voices inside the hotel's hallway. Sticking his head out, he asked one of the occupants what was going on. "They say the Horace Mann High School is on fire!" Stewart ran down the hallway and joined a small crowd of onlookers viewing out the window. The darkened sky now emitted a bright orange glow that half the population of Marion watched in horror.

CHAPTER 6

Actual photo of the Horace Mann High School fire carnage

Early the following morning, crime scene investigator Captain Benjamin Stewart was on hand at the scene of the previous night's terrible fire. The Marion Fire Department had fought a gallant battle to extinguish the blazing inferno. The interior rubble was still too hot for any type of investigation to commence. If the school had to burn, it was lucky for everyone to do so at night and not endanger human life. The police were doing their best to hold back the crowds of curious onlookers and students who naturally sought to see what had occurred.

The mayor of the city was on hand and boasted that the school would be rebuilt before the start of a new fall school year. Some who heard his statement wondered if that was even possible, due to the extent of the damages.

Investigator's assistant Hugo Barns caught the eye of Stewart and motioned for him to come to that location. Several policemen were standing about looking down at something on the ground that Stewart couldn't make out. It proved to be two empty cans that were assumed to have held kerosene due to their faint odor. Laying close by was what appeared to be a lab or doctor's white coat, now badly soiled. "Touch nothing until the photographer arrives," Stewart instructed the police officers. One of the policemen then went in search of the photographer who was already on-site taking pictures and instructed him to follow. After ensuring photos had been taken of the discovery, Stewart gave instructions to Hugo for the careful removal of the cans and to check them for fingerprints. The aid then left. Stewart began to examine the white coat and noticed the owner's name, Andrews, on the label. After a quick check of the pockets, the typed letter was discovered and its interesting contents read. With the letter and coat in hand, Stewart made his way over to a small group of people. One he recognized as the vice-principal, Victor Stanton. The man had watery eyes but did his best not to allow them to show to anyone. "Mr. Stanton, I'm Captain Stewart. Would you mind stepping over here where we may speak privately?" He then did so.

"This is horrible! Our beautiful school is destroyed. Have they found out what caused it, Captain?" Stanton asked.

"I wouldn't know, sir. It's just too early to tell. I want to ask you a question. Are the names, Barney and Lisa familiar to you? I must insist that anything we speak about here be kept strictly confidential."

"We have a science teacher, the one that was shot at a couple of weeks ago, Barnaby Andrews. As for Lisa, the only female instructor we have of that name is Mrs. Lisa McCormick. Why? Are they connected with this fire?"

"I cannot comment on that, sir, but thank you for your assistance."

"Well Captain, if you're looking for Mr. Andrews, he's standing over there with a few teachers and students," he said, pointing in the direction of a group of onlookers. Stanton turned towards the charred remains and said to no one in particular, "I pray that we may rebuild it as quickly as possible." Steward wished for that as well as he walked toward the assembled group.

Stewart had not met Andrews during the shooting investigation but spotted him based on the description he already had of the man. "Let's talk," Stewart softly said as he motioned the young teacher away. "Mr. Andrews, I'm Captain Stewart from the Grant County Sheriff's Department and I need to ask you a few questions. Can you identify this for me?" He then handed the lab coat to Andrews. After a brief examination, the teacher stated it was his lab coat from the chemistry lab.

"How did you obtain it, sir?"

"It was found outside of the school, along with two empty containers of what appears to have contained kerosene." Stewart was a master at detecting deception in the face and mannerisms of suspects, and he watched intently for the reaction.

"But.. how did my coat..." Andrews said in surprise.

"Did you set fire to the school, Mr. Andrews?"

"What! Me? No! I set no fire! I would never do such a terrible thing!" Andrews was most adamant in his denial.

"I think you need to come down to the office with me Mr. Andrews. I have a few more questions to ask," Stewart said.

"Am I under some kind of arrest?" The man pleaded.

"No, we just need to get a few more things straightened out. Come along now, sir."

From a distance, Chad McCormick watched intently as he saw a lawman escorting Barnaby Andrews off, hopefully to the county jail for questioning. "I hope they hang the guy," he said out loud in pure excitement. So far, his plan was working perfectly. He then returned to his office.

* * * * * * * * *

"I tell you, I don't know how my lab coat found its way next to those cans. I swear to you, I had nothing to do with this. Someone is trying to frame me. Someone's already taken a shot at me." He then reached into his pocket. "Here is the key to my room at Keller's Boarding House. Take it and go inside. There you'll find two threatening letters I received from someone called The Scorpion. That's the person you should be after, not me! I was in bed by ten o'clock last night. Go ask my landlady. I said goodnight to her before I retired."

"We've already interviewed her and have the two letters," Steward said. "Who do you think this Scorpion is?"

"For the life of me, I don't know. I've racked my brain trying to figure it out."

Now Stewart intended to change the subject. "Why would this Scorpion take a shot at you, Mr. Andrews? Perhaps fooling around with another man's wife, maybe?"

"No!"

"I think you need to explain something we found in the pocket of your lab coat." Rather than hand a piece of evidence over, Stewart read it aloud.

"That's a dirty lie! I have never acted inappropriately with Mrs. McCormick! She never sent me any such thing; I swear it on my mother's grave!" Hugo Barns who had sat in on the questioning looked up at Stewart and slightly nodded his head, indicating he believed the man's story.

"Alright Mr. Andrews, you can go home now. Just don't leave the city. If we need to question you further, we know where to find you," Stewart said. The very relieved man quickly left for home.

Back at their office, Stewart continued, "I think he's telling the truth. All along my gut was telling me this case against him was just too pat. How convenient to find the incriminating evidence right at the scene of the crime. Someone is framing him for some reason."

"Another officer tapped on the door and entered. "Someone wiped off all the fingerprints on the kerosene cans." He then left the room.

"That clinches it," Stewart said. "Would someone go to great lengths to rid any fingerprints from the cans used at the fire, but be foolish enough to leave his lab coat and letter inside the pocket? No way. Andrews isn't our man, but somebody had gone to great lengths to implicate him. Hugo, what do we have on Mr. and Mrs. McCormick?"

"He owns McCormick Power & Light company. She was a teacher, at least until last night, at the high school. She is a pretty little thing too. Should we look into the adultery charge?"

"No, my friend. That's not our job or we might have to investigate a large chunk of the local population," he chuckled. "Who is this Scorpion person, and why do they have it in for Andrews, or the husband and wife? Go see Mrs. McCormick and see what she has to say about this. Later we'll go speak with her husband at work."

"Is it alright to mention the contents of the letter?" Stewart replied yes to do so. Hugo nodded, grabbed his hat, and left.

CHAPTER 7

The Interviews

Hugo Barns arrived at the home of Mr. and Mrs. McCormick and knocked. Lisa opened the door, and by the look of her, she'd been crying. "Mrs. McCormick? I'm Investigating Assistant Hugo Barns of the Grant County Sheriff's Department. May I come in?"

"Oh, alright. Come," she replied as she wiped her eyes with a handkerchief. "Have they determined the cause of the fire? This is a terrible loss and I'm heartbroken over it. Thank God our children were safe at home."

"Yes ma'am, but that's not why I'm here today. I need to ask you a few questions."

"Sure. I'll assist you in any way I can."

"Mrs. McCormick, do you know a Barnaby Andrews?"

"Yes, of course. He's our science and biology teacher. Why? He's not hurt or anything, is he?" Hugo ignored her question.

"What is your relationship with Mr. Andrews?"

"Relationship? Barney is a great friend, if that's what you mean. All the students love him."

"Were you in love with him also?"

Annoyance appeared upon her face. "What are you insinuating, sir? I'm a married woman!"

"We have discovered a typed letter addressed to him from you breaking off an illicit affair."

"What! I wrote no such letter! We are only coworkers at school."

"I hate to ask you this ma'am, but would you say your marriage is solid?"

Her delay in answering provided the answer. "Well...my husband is the jealous type...and for some reason..he's got it in his head that I have been unfaithful with Mr. Andrews. I can assure you I have had no relationship beyond friendship with that man. I can't believe you're even asking me these personal and insulting questions!"

"I'm sorry ma'am, it's just part of my job and I assure you it has a direct correlation with a criminal investigation. So, would you say your husband exhibits hatred toward Mr. Andrews?" Lisa McCormick slowly nodded. "I'm afraid he does."

"Does the name 'Scorpion' mean anything to you?"

"Well, yes. You see my husband grew up in Arizona and is always talking about those creepy things. I've never seen one in person, but the thought of one crawling about gives me the jitters."

"Does your husband possess any firearms?"

"Yes, he has some sort of rifle. It's there in the back of the coat closet. I don't like guns, but it had belonged to his father and..."

"Would you mind if I examined it?"

"No sir, feel free to do so."

Hugo opened the closet and rummaged about. "There isn't any rifle in here," he stated.

"Are you sure?" She then began to search the closet. "That's strange, it's gone."

Hugo thanked her for her time and hurried back to inform Captain Stewart of the developments he had just learned.

* * * * * * * * *

Captain Stewart was very interested in learning what his friend had uncovered. "Chad McCormick seems to have the motive to attempt to murder Mr. Andrews. As for the fire, I haven't heard anything yet from Assistant Fire Chief Dupont, but I would assume arson is highly likely. Let's pay a visit to Mr. McCormick and see what he has to say." The pair left and took Stewart's 1904 Studebaker to the office of McCormick's Power & Light.

Office Manager Lawrence Fields was on the telephone speaking with another disgruntled customer when the two men entered. "We're from the Sheriff's Department and need to speak with Mr. Chad McCormick." Fields pointed toward the boss's office and continued to listen to the customer on the other end of the line, though it was now too difficult to concentrate. *It's a good sign when the law comes to question that little weasel!*

Both officers walked straight into Chad McCormick's office unannounced. The owner was sitting behind his desk looking over the company's payroll ledger. "Mr. McCormick?

I'm Captain Stewart from the Grant County Sheriff's Office. This is Inspector Barns. We would like to ask you a few questions."

Chad froze momentarily in place before pointing to two nearby chairs. "Please, have a seat. How may I help you, gentlemen?"

"I'll come right to the point," Stewart said. "What do you know about the school fire that occurred last night?"

"Well, I saw the flames and all. You see, my wife is a school teacher there and..."

Stewart's attention had diverted from the man's response to something else. He sensed that Hugo had noticed it also. What they each detected was the distinct odor of kerosene. "Mr. McCormick, I need to ask you to come around to the front of the desk, sir." Chad thought it was a very odd request but complied. As soon as he did, Hugo dropped down to his knees and placed his nose above the man's shoes. Chad froze in panic. *They must smell something! Why didn't I think to change my shoes?* Hugo looked up and nodded to Stewart.

"How did you get the odor of kerosene on your shoes, Mr. McCormick?" Stewart wanted to know.

"I...I don't know. I must have stepped in something this morning," he offered in reply.

"Please remove both of your shoes," Stewart demanded. Knowing he had no other option but to comply, Chad returned to his seat and sat down. While removing each shoe, he casually attempted to brush away some of the dark powder he noticed on each heal. His actions were seen by both lawmen. "I'll take them," Hugo said.

"Do you have an office typewriter?"

"Yes, it's out in the office manager's room." By now Chad was beginning to sweat. *What am I going to do? They suspect I set the fire. I would have thought the faint odor would have dissipated before now.*

Stewart informed the office manager that the typewriter was to be held in evidence and asked if he'd mind carrying it outside and placing it inside his car. Fields replied he'd be honored to do so. "Is this the only office typewriter?" Hugo asked.

"Yes, sir, it most certainly is."

"You're going to have to come with us Mr. McCormick to answer a few more questions back at the office," Stewart stated.

"In my stocking feet?" McCormick asked. Neither officer replied. As the small automobile pulled away, a grinning Lawrence Fields waved a hearty goodbye.

* * * * * * * * *

Two hours later...

Chad McCormick was in trouble. He was in deep trouble. After a closer examination, his shoes were found to contain particles of coal dust as well as kerosene. Also, the typewriter font from the office typewriter matched perfectly with the letter discovered inside the lab coat. Someone in that office typed it out and it now appeared it was Chad McCormick. Changing the subject, he was asked, "By the way, do you own a weapon, a rifle perhaps?"

The question seemed out of the ordinary. "Why yes, I inherited a Winchester Model 73 from my father."

"That's a nice rifle. What caliber shell does it take?"

"44-40. It's a lever-action model and a real beauty."

"When was the last time you fired it?" Now Chad was suspicious as to where all of the was going.

"Sometime last fall, I think. Why are you asking these stupid questions?"

Hugo said, "I had an interesting discussion with your wife earlier today. She told me of your intense jealousy of Barnaby Andrews. Is that why you tried to shoot him?"

"I did no such thing! I heard talk of the shooting, but I know nothing about it."

"Where is your rifle now?"

"In the back of our coat closet, standing up on the left corner wall."

"No, it's not there, and you know where you put it after you shot at Mr. Andrews. Come clean now and admit you tried to kill him. We already have a firm case against you for starting the high school fire." Seeing now that his situation was hopeless, Chad McCormick finally admitted setting the fire and attempting to place the blame on Barnaby Andrews.

"But I had absolutely nothing to do at all with trying to kill him. It's true I hate his guts and wish whoever did was a better shot. It was probably another woman's husband. But I have no idea where my rifle is. There are hundreds of models just like it in town anyway." Stewart and Barns were quite happy to obtain the arson confession but disappointed the man hadn't admitted to the shooting. McCormick was correct on one thing, there were hundreds of models just like it in Marion's homes. Without the rifle in hand, there could be no ballistics check with the fragment removed from the wall. A stenographer was then called in and took down his confession.

"We're placing you under arrest Mr. McCormick on suspicion of arson," Captain Stewart said. The prisoner was then booked. Chad would have many nights behind bars to contemplate his foul deeds. The following day, his attorney introduced a motion to have the case transferred to Kokomo as there was little chance for his client to obtain a fair trial in Marion. For some reason, the local citizens resented anyone charged with destroying their high school building. The motion was granted by the judge and the prisoner was soon transferred to the Kokomo jail to await trial.

* * * * * * * * *

Late Saturday Night...

Within a darkened bedroom, two sweaty bodies had just completed another act of love-making. Lisa McCormick lay exhausted but quite content. The man reached over and pulled her close as he kissed her cheek and brushed away the strands of hair that had covered her face. He knew to arrive at her home well after everyone was expected to be off of the streets and must be gone once again well before daylight. Lisa said, "I am so happy now that everything has fallen into place. Our plans appear to have had a mind of its own and now I'm rid of that stupid husband once and for all. The love poem you wrote to me had set everything in motion and Chad naturally assumed it to be Barney Andrews, just like I hoped. Now everything will belong to me and the divorce papers are being processed on Monday by my new lawyer."

The man she was speaking to...her lover and fellow conspirator...was fireman Brian O'Brian. He replied, "Yes, and after using my gloves so as not to leave fingerprints on your husband's rifle, I stalked Andrews out and fired the shot, purposely missing as you made me promise to do. Later I planned to shoot him in the leg and then leave the rifle where it would be found and analyzed. That would have put him straight into jail. But all that changed when he went a bit crazy and wrote those threatening Scorpion letters. That told the cops someone was definitely after Andrews and your soon-to-be-ex-hubby walked right into the trap."

"I knew he'd been searching my room, so I dug out an old locket that my parents gave me and placed it in my purse. It was engraved *Forever* and that was the final straw that pushed him over. It worked so wonderfully, but I've got to admit, it almost threw me when that cop came by and said they had a letter that I supposedly typed to Andrews. I played it cool and relied on the acting skills I'd developed in college drama class. I never dreamed he was crazy enough to burn down our school. Anyway, it all worked out just as I hoped so you can get up now and leave. I'm through with you for good."

Brian could hardly believe his ears. "What? I thought you loved me...and that we would be together forever. That's why I agreed to help you, sweetheart. I love you!"

"I used you to get what I wanted like I've used other men before. Now we're finished and by the way, don't forget that it was YOU that shot at Andrews and was behind the entire scheme to break up my marriage for your own evil intentions. If you make trouble, it will be you that goes to jail, not me. I'm just a poor unfortunate woman whose husband went crazy. People will believe me and not you. So go, get out, and if we ever meet on the street, remember I don't even know you!"

Brian O'Brian realized he had been duped by an expert. He dressed and left with his mind trying to come to grips with this new reality.

* * * * * * * * *

On Monday morning, Lawrence Fields approached Lisa McCormick with an offer to purchase the business. He offered a low figure, thinking she would be thrilled to rid herself of a business she knew nothing about. Instead, she informed him that his service was no longer needed and that SHE would run McCormick's Power & Light herself. Lawrence Fields was shocked to discover that the love-letter campaign he'd supplied to her husband had not produced the results intended. The following day, Fields cleaned out his desk and obtained his last paycheck. That afternoon, now ex-school teacher Lisa McCormick moved into her husband's office. She immediately made friends with the three electrical workmen, using her well-rehearsed female charms, and promised each a small raise if they would remain and help guide her until she learned the business. Once everyone got over the shock of having a new woman boss, all agreed to remain and help. The bookkeeping part of her job proved to be quite easy and after a few mistakes in ordering the wrong materials, she finally got a solid hold on the business. Wives were quick to recommend her company to their husbands for all electrical needs. McCormick's Power & Light became successful.

* * * * * * * * *

The Curse of the Hanging Tree

Three months later Chad McCormick went on trial. The evidence against him was overwhelming and he was sentenced to a long prison term. Every day he relived that terrible night and wished he had found a better way of punishing his cheating wife and her boyfriend, Barnaby Andrews.

* * * * * * * * *

Life indeed prospered for Lisa McCormick and along with it, a successful climb up the social ladder. She now found herself invited to events she had previously only dreamed about. Younger and older wealthy men began to show great interest in her and in time, Lisa hoped to marry again and continue her upward climb as far as she could reach. In October, Lisa sent out invitations to her prominent friends to attend her masquerade Halloween Party, to be held at her new luxurious home. That evening men and women, wearing all kinds of masks and costumes, began arriving. Her ballroom was quickly filling with important people and Lisa was having the time of her life when a muffled "pop" was heard. Pandemonium quickly broke out as the party's hostess, Lisa McCormick, slumped to the floor quite dead. Later, someone said they thought they saw a man dressed in a fireman's costume leaving the scene. The shooter was never caught and the murder of Lisa McCormick was never solved. Upon notification that his wife had been murdered, Chad McCormick laughed and shouted that justice had finally been served.

The End

Please consider reading any of my other books if you have enjoyed these stories. The following pages contain each book's cover as well as a brief synopsis. My books may be purchased from Amazon.com or I keep a small amount here at my home for local pickup. Drop by and say hello.

Alan E Losure

The Curse of the Hanging Tree

HISTORICAL TIDBITS OF LOCAL INTEREST ON MARION, INDIANA

Horace Mann High School, located between Third and Fourth Street, did catch fire, four times to be exact. The years were 1902, 1906, 1908, and 1923.

The city of Marion received its first motorized fire truck around 1915 and was housed in the station at Third Street and Western Avenue. The pattern for its radiator top was made at the Marion Malleable Iron Works. The old newspaper image I was able to obtain was too dark to print here, but the article named the truck driver to be Henry Snyder. Also present are fellow firemen Charles Case and Thomas Hamilton. Two years later the department became fully mechanized. The firemen of the past were a brave lot, just as today's firefighters. We thank you for your service.

Marion City Hall was located at Fourth and Boots Street.

The Hyers Comedy Company arrived in Marion and were taken to the Brunswick lodging home, where their advanced agent had secured a signed contract. What was not known to the proprietor at the signing was that the company's members were Negros. He immediately attempted to stop their entry until reminded of the signed contract. The man could provide no other reason for his actions, except based on race, which he called "the color line." Once reluctantly admitted, the group attempted to eat at a local café but were told they had to wait until his other customers were served. This would not do and the group was directed to another local café where they and their money were welcomed.

In the year 1890, a deranged serial killer imitating London's infamous Jack the Ripper is at large within the small Indiana towns of Jonesboro and Harrisburg (Gas City). Using the name "Son of Jack" women of all ages are being mutilated while leaving no clues behind. Can Jonesboro's Marshal Livingston bring an end to this senseless reign of terror before the evil Son of Jack strikes again?

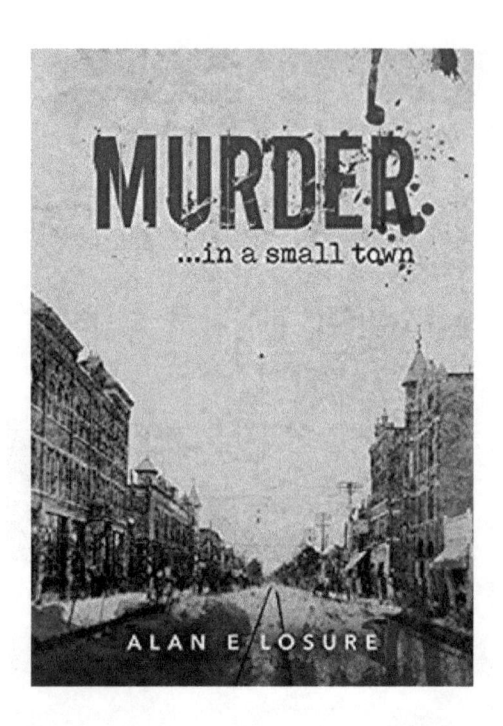

It was well after midnight when the group of four met inside the darkened storage barn one-half mile north of town. Each arrived quietly knowing that new business was at hand that would require swift justice. No names were ever spoken though the identity of everyone was known but never discussed. A barn lantern was lit and the evening activities were discussed. They met not to represent the local law enforcement community but to avenge the guilty and the transgressors as they saw fit to do whether Negro, white man, or woman. Justice will be served this night by the terrorist group known as the White Caps.

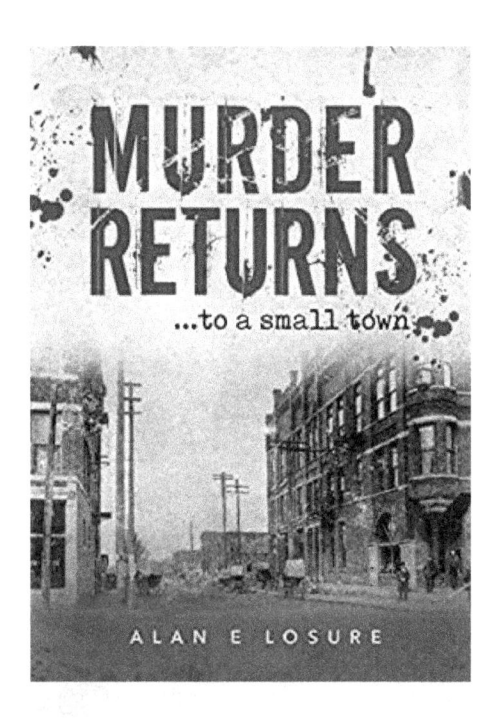

Saloon woman Maggie O'Shea was in a total panic having discovered early this morning; a warning note laid by the doorway with a rock holding it from blowing away. Though moisture had made some of the blurred words hard to read, Maggie had no difficulty understanding a threat when she saw it. By now everyone in Gas City knew of the 13th Disciple and that he backs up his threats using biblical quotes to justify murder.

The note read:

Leviticus 24:15-16 *"Say to the Israelites: If anyone curses his God, he will be held responsible; anyone who blasphemes the name of the Lord must be put to death." The entire assembly must stone him.*

Ezekiel 16: 35 *"Wherefore, O harlot, hear the word of the Lord."*

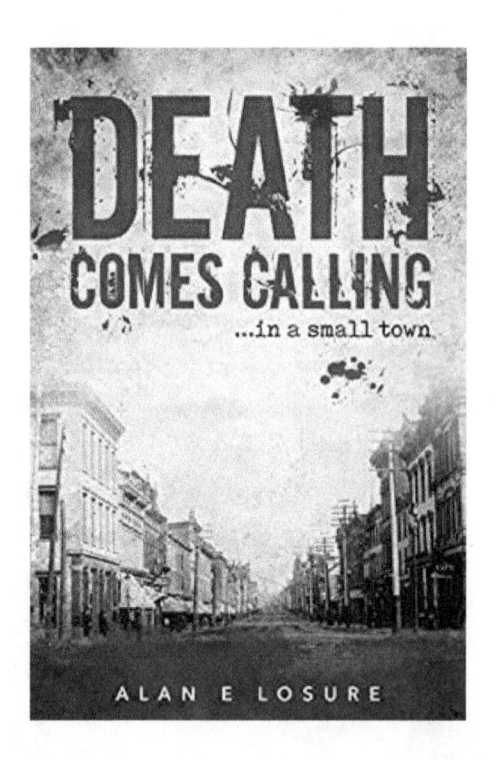

In the year 1896, pure evil stalked the land. Tom and Jack Milford were soon to be rich men by their standards. "Please," the farm wife begged, "Don't hit my husband anymore. I'll tell...I'll tell," she screamed. "There's a loose floorboard under the table and a cash box is hidden under it. Please tell me my husband is alright!"

Knowing that her husband was already dead, Jack lied, "He'll be alright now that you've told us about the money." Assured that this was all the family possessed, it was now time to have a little more fun. Shoving the chair with Mrs. Johnston now securely tied up to the front of the fireplace, Jack forced the bottom legs of the chair with her legs and bare feet into the flames..

The Curse of the Hanging Tree

THE MYSTERY OF THE TOLLING BELL

ALAN E. LOSURE

During the early-morning hours of 1898 in the small community of Gas City, Indiana, a strange, mournful sound of thirteen bell tolls was heard coming from the high school's bell tower. How the tolling could be accomplished inside a locked building was not known. At the same time, the body of a young man, a recent high school graduate, was discovered. Many wondered if the haunting spirit of 'Gary the Ghost', who died at the school under mysterious circumstances, was signaling his final acts of revenge against the Class of '98. It was now up to Marshal Justin Blake and his deputies to unravel this ghastly murder and bring about the capture of the killer - be it man or spirit.

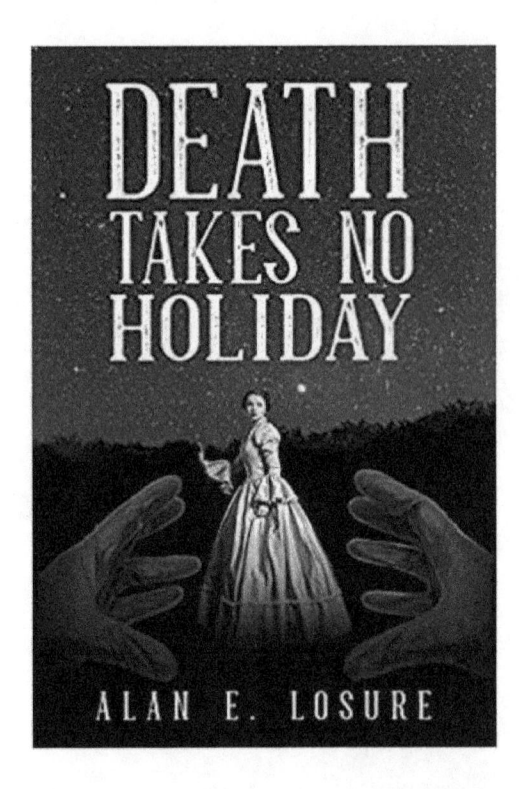

In the year 1898, a fiendish figure labeled "The Night Stalker" began terrorizing the small community of Gas City, Indiana, murdering young and old alike, while leaving no clues behind. As intense community pressure mounted, it was up to Marshal Justin Blake and his deputies to apprehend this evil perpetrator before another innocent victim fell to its clutches. Otherwise, the threat of lawless vigilante justice will become a reality.

The Curse of the Hanging Tree

In the year 1900, Indiana author Albert Larson published his newest murder-mystery novel: The Copycat Killer. Within the pages, a fictional author is murdered by an unknown person who uses the book's name as their own and employs the story's seven threats to kill people in town.

Soon after, a real-life drama occurs when Larson is murdered, using the same exact threats outlined in the novel and using the book's title, The Copycat Killer, as their own. It falls to Marshal Justin Blake to catch this crazed killer before the threats to murder scores of other people become a reality.

Alan E. Losure

With the recent discovery of an old diary belonging to a young girl captured by Ho-Chunk Indians in 1827, retired postmaster Frank Meadows, his grandson Parker, and a group of professional Wisconsin researchers set out to uncover the truth behind the disappearance of a party of U.S. Army personnel, lost somewhere in the Great American Northwest Territory. According to the diary, a payroll chest of early-American silver coinage may be buried somewhere near Wisconsin's Lake Winnebago. Can this treasure be located after nearly two hundred years? And if so, what unique secret lies buried within its content.

In the year 1887, the 'Go-Devil Killer' is terrorizing the small community of Fairmount, Indiana using a supply of stolen nitroglycerin to kill and put out of business a family-owned natural gas company. It quickly falls upon Marshal Caleb Web and Deputy Tony Angelo to do everything possible to end this terrible reign of terror once and for all before more innocent lives perish at the hands of this fiendish murderer.

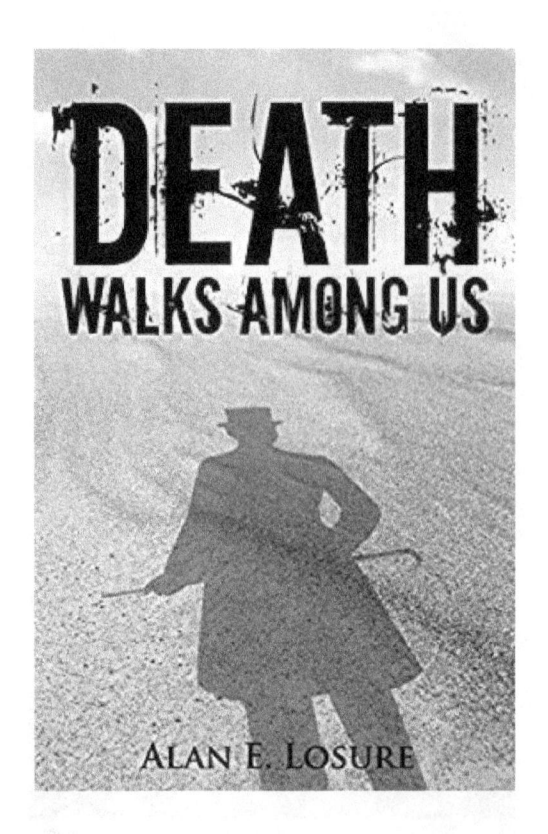

In the year 1889, a young girl by the name of Nancy Hamilton arrived with her family in the small town of Fairmount, Indiana with what seemingly was a gift of prophecy, reciting poems that foretell upcoming horrible deaths. Is she a witch as many claimed or blessed by a Heavenly Spirit? What is the truth behind her unique ability to predict the future? It's now up to Marshal Caleb Webb and his deputies to solve what lies behind her powers and end the reign of murders once and for all.

QUEST FOR THE TRUTH

ALAN E. LOSURE

Loneliness was the worst part of his life now. The days were long but the nights even longer. If he was ever going to accomplish that which his inner voice had instructed him to do, that which he had planned to do someday, he needed to make up his mind and do it now. He had known many yesterdays and expected few tomorrows. Pausing briefly to compose his private thoughts, the old man began to write.

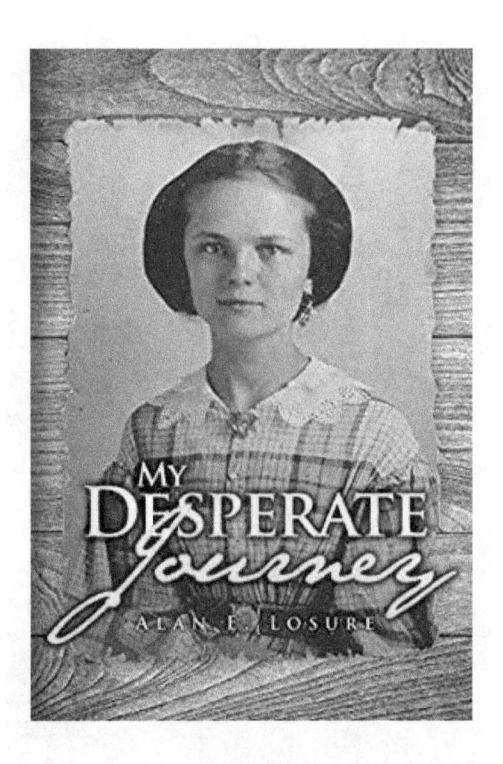

"The freight car doors were opened, and planks were laid to force all of the women and children to walk up and enter the cars. There were no seats, and each car was packed tightly with our people. Mother, Vicki, and I managed to stay together, and we soon found ourselves jammed in tightly, like pigs going to slaughter. Before closing and locking the open doorway, a Union soldier placed a wooden bucket inside and instructed that it be placed in a corner. This bucket was our only latrine for all of us to use. He then gave us a bucket of water and a box of army biscuits that was meant to last everyone for the long journey. We begged him not to close the door, but soon found ourselves in near darkness as the train began to move northward."

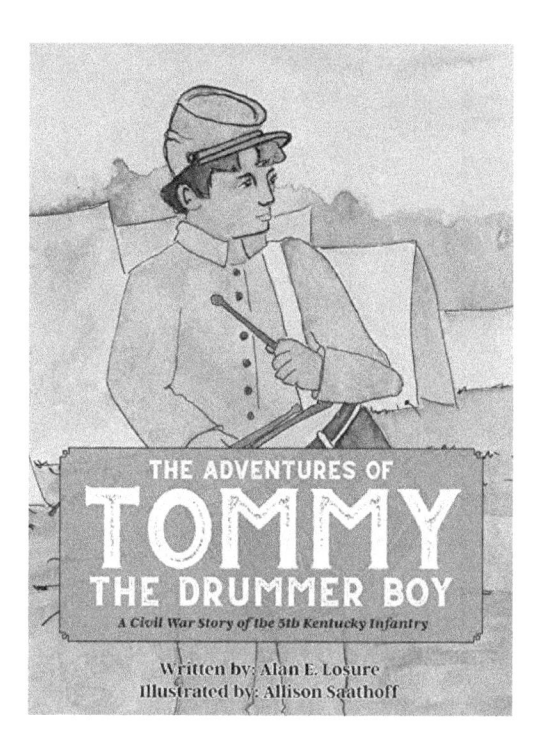

These are the exciting adventures of young Tommy Lee who became a Confederate drummer boy in the 5th Kentucky Infantry. Tommy will share with you his many experiences and the life-long friends he made along the way during the Civil War. Beautifully illustrated. Suggested ages: 7-10 years.